Cody

Cody

An American Extreme Bull Riders Tour Romance

Megan Crane

Cody

Tule Publishing First Printing, May 2017
The Tule Publishing Group, LLC

ISBN: 978-1-946772-65-7

Chapter One

"I'M SO SORRY," the woman said, instead of hello.

Just like the last three women before her.

Skylar Grey was tired of *sorry*. She was tired of being treated as if she might break into pieces at any moment. Or as if she was already in pieces and the lack of an instant *I'm sorry* might reduce her to dust, right there where she stood in a happy blue sundress that was significantly more cheerful than she felt.

She'd been tired of the compulsory sympathy for at least the last eighteen months, and yet it continued. It always, always continued. It defied space and time. It had followed her from Georgia to Montana and showed no signs of stopping.

The truth was, she was fed up with condolences. But short of changing her name and disappearing, she didn't know how to make them stop.

"You poor, poor thing," continued the woman in Skylar's father's backyard, completely unaware that her perfectly kind gesture was putting Skylar's teeth on edge.

Skylar didn't know this woman. This was her father's

annual Fourth of July party, to which he invited most of Billings, Montana, and any of his customers in the surrounding area, and Skylar hadn't lived in Billings since she'd left town for college at eighteen. She hadn't expected to know anyone. It was one of the main reasons she'd moved home, in fact.

But it didn't matter. Everybody seemed to know her.

"I'm so impressed with you," the woman was saying in a confiding tone. Her brow wrinkled and her eyes widened in that same *deeply sympathetic* expression that Skylar had seen, almost without exception, on every face in her vicinity for over two years. "I think I would just curl up in the fetal position for years."

Skylar was aware of the endless expanse of the Montana sky above her, the hot summer sun giving way to a deep blue evening. She swirled her drink in its plastic cup, wishing she had the head for the strong stuff. And more, wishing she could just open her mouth and let all the things that jostled around inside of her come on out and jostle at this woman instead.

She did not say, *You should have seen me right after he died. I don't think I moved for weeks.* She did not say, *You would be surprised what you can handle when you have to.* This woman barely knew Skylar. She certainly didn't know Thayer. If anything, she knew the same story that everyone seemed to, that local sporting goods king Billy Grey's eldest daughter's fiancé had been killed in a drunk-driving accident two years ago. Just a simple little sentence to encompass the sudden end of Thayer's life and everything that had died with him, like all the plans and dreams he'd shared with Skylar. Like the life Skylar had been living up until that point.

This woman didn't deserve to know real things about Skylar or Skylar's actual feelings or a single thing about the life of a good man when all she'd ever know about Thayer Sexton was his death.

Skylar managed to refrain from telling the woman that it wasn't *Billy Grey's daughter* she was trying to comfort in the middle of a party, but herself. She didn't point out that if she had a penny for all the times people had told her what they imagined they'd do if they were unlucky enough to be her, she would be a very rich woman. Rich enough to go live on a private island somewhere instead of in her childhood bedroom in her father's house, where she could make certain no one offered her any more condolences as long as she drew breath.

Instead of sharing any of that, she did what she always did.

"Thank you," she said solemnly, and smiled—a little bit sadly. She'd become an expert at this particular smile. A solemn curve of her lips, no dimple, and some frank eye contact. Her sister Scottie had cackled and called it her *widow smile* last Christmas. Even if, technically, Skylar wasn't a widow since Thayer had died four months before their wedding. "You're very kind."

She moved away before the woman could move on to more inappropriate questions and comments, because she knew that was the next step. It was always the next step. Because humans in general were really bad with grief.

It was yet another lesson Skylar hadn't wanted to learn, but she had. Just like the rest of them, whether she'd wanted to or not.

She kept her smile welded to her mouth as she made her way through the crowd, stopping only briefly by the drinks table to swipe herself a cold bottle of water. She could hear her father's laugh winding through the throng, and smiled a little more naturally at the sound before she ducked in the back door and sighed as a blast of air conditioning washed over her.

She'd missed that laugh. She'd missed her father, her family, and the whole state of Montana, it turned out. Leaving Atlanta had seemed crazy to everyone she'd known there. They knew her from her college days at the University of Georgia out in Athens, or from all those post-collegiate years in Atlanta in the same sprawling group of people where she and Thayer had met, become friends, and then gradually turned into more than friends.

You're moving to Montana? Her former college roommate Shelby had stared at her over lunch as if Skylar had said she was relocating to Mars. *To* Montana, *of all places?*

I'm from Montana, Skylar had reminded her, because no

one seemed to remember that. It was possible Skylar had downplayed it herself, all those years ago, in her eagerness to fit in down south.

If her friends had been flabbergasted, Thayer's family had acted as if she'd betrayed them. His mother had sat in the sprawling Ansley Park mansion where Thayer had been raised and wept openly. His sisters had looked at Skylar as if she was the devil sent to harm them. Even his father, never given to shows of anything like emotion when a certain boisterous charm would do, had struggled to hide his disappointment.

I guess we didn't think you'd want *to move on with your life so soon,* he'd said eventually.

As if it was two hours after Thayer's funeral instead of two years.

And Skylar hadn't actually known if she was doing the right thing. How could she? She'd thrown herself, heart and soul, into the life she'd built in Georgia. And she'd met Thayer three days after moving to Atlanta with her best friends from UGA. There wasn't a single part of her life there that wasn't haunted by his loss. She couldn't go anywhere without running into people, places, things, that brought it all back. It had gotten to the point where she'd holed up in the apartment she'd shared with him instead of going out to face the sympathy, which in turn had made it seem as if she was hiding herself away, presumably wrapped in a shroud.

The funny thing was how many people clearly wanted

that to be true, because if she ever emerged—shroudless—they didn't like it. It was clear that Skylar was considered a walking, talking shrine to Thayer. Everyone who had known him needed her to be that and nothing else.

For a while she'd needed that, too.

And in the end, it had been easier to leave Atlanta than she'd ever imagined it could have been back when Thayer was alive and all of their dreams involved staying put right there in his beloved hometown.

But that didn't mean moving back home had been the right thing to do. The truth was, Skylar was as trapped here as she'd been in Atlanta.

Her brother Jesse had actually moved himself to call her when he'd heard, instead of sending her his usual random texts.

Tell me you are not moving in with Dad, he'd said with the brusqueness she imagined served him well as some construction tycoon or other out there in Seattle.

I am. Skylar had been packing up the last of her things and had paused to look out her window as the Midtown neighborhood she'd loved so much hustled along out there in the sweltering June humidity without her. *Why not? I thought things were okay between the two of you.*

Things had not been okay for years after Jesse had brought his girlfriend home for Christmas one year and their father had poached her, making Angelique his third wife even though she was basically his daughters' age. But then

Jesse had met Michaela, the woman he was marrying at the end of July, and it had been forgiveness all around. Or so he'd said.

We're fine, Jesse had said then. *But you're obviously not thinking straight if you want to go back to Billings and reenact high school.*

I liked high school, she pointed out, and had laughed when he'd made a rude noise.

Jesse hated Billings. Skylar would have said he hated Montana altogether if that wasn't impossible. They were Greys. Montana was bred into their bones and had been since the first Grey had found his way into the Wild West in the late 1800s, leaving some or other scandal behind in Massachusetts. What Jesse had really hated was their father, even before the Angelique thing. Skylar had always thought that was what had made her brother so driven. He'd put himself through college and became a wild success out in Seattle, mostly so he could prove that he didn't need any part of their father's regional sporting goods empire.

It meant was that Jesse wasn't necessarily the best judge about thinking straight when it came to going home. He was a lot more like their mother, who had taken her divorce from their cheating father so hard that she'd remained an angry hermit ever since. Not because she was so broken up about it, Skylar and Scottie had always agreed privately, but because Carolyn Evers—no longer Carolyn Grey—wanted her enduring solitude to stand as a monument to Billy's faithlessness.

That was a whole lot of hate and Skylar just didn't have it in her.

And anyway, she'd known she'd done the right thing before she'd even landed at the Billings airport.

Eastern Montana had sprawled there below her, gold and blue and as perfect as she'd remembered it in all these years of only coming home in the Christmas snow, and her heart had lifted in a way she'd thought it never would again. And the drive to her father's house on that pretty June afternoon had made her almost giddy; it was so good to be back beneath the great arc of the endless sky, with hardy, pretty Billings stretched out before her like a welcome mat.

She was still happy she wasn't in Atlanta anymore, she told herself now. Skylar stood in the great room of her father's sprawling but cozy ranch house, enjoying the air conditioning and the break from the party outside that was as much a business function as anything else. But over the past month she'd discovered that even the last, best place that would always be home to her didn't keep people from treating her as if she'd died right along with Thayer two years back.

As if she was nothing more than a ghost.

Still.

The doorbell jolted her out of another round of unproductive thoughts, and the uncomfortable realization she'd been putting off for just about a month now. Which was that she needed to go somewhere no one knew her. She needed to find a place where her past was something she got to share only when and if she wanted. Where no one expected her to grieve or considered her a shrine or thought that any gesture she made toward the life Thayer would never have was a betrayal of him.

Because if she didn't, she might as well have jumped into Thayer's grave right along with him. Sometimes she worried she had. Sometimes she dreamed it, entirely too vividly, and woke in her tidy little childhood bedroom gasping for air as if she was being buried alive.

As if no matter where she went, she stayed trapped.

Skylar tried to shake that off as she walked down the hall toward the front door. Her father had been nice enough to make a space for her, in his house and in his business, and she couldn't just disappear on him because it didn't feel the way she'd hoped it would. His sporting goods chain was sponsoring the American Extreme Bull Riders Tour when it rolled into town this coming weekend, and she knew he needed her to work the event. There would be no throwing pins at maps and flouncing off somewhere new, no matter how appealing an idea it was.

At least, not yet.

Sometimes Skylar couldn't tell if her heart was irreparably broken or if she simply had a new heart now, and it yearned for things she didn't know how to name.

She swung open her father's front door, smiled automatically at the hat and the crisp jeans that shouted *cowboy,* and then took a closer look. And went very, very still.

Because the man who loomed there, his face hard and unsmiling as he held his cowboy hat in one big hand, made the heart she wasn't sure she knew anymore kick. Hard. Then again.

"I'm looking for Billy Grey," he said, in the kind of low, dark voice that made every last part of Skylar demand she…*do something.*

He looked like every daydream she'd ever had of a cowboy, and then some. His jeans clung to solid thighs and his belt buckle gleamed. His boots were polished to a high sheen. *Bull rider,* something in her whispered, because he had that look, though he was tall for a sport that tended to favor slighter, more wiry men who could keep their balance on the backs of ornery, bucking animals. Everything about the way he stood, from the loose-limbed ease to the set of his wide shoulders, told her he was competent and confident in all things. Unflappable, as a man who tested himself against giant bulls would have to be. Ready no matter what, come what may. His button-down shirt was tucked in, but managed to cling to the lean, muscled expanse of his chest. His dirty blond hair looked a little messy, as if he spent more time raking his fingers through it than worrying about it, and he had the makings of a five-o'clock shadow on his square jaw as it was coming up on a bright summer seven p.m.

And his dark green gaze was uncompromisingly direct.

It made something deep inside of her shake itself to life, then curl into a hot little knot of pure sensation.

"He's out in back," Skylar heard herself say in a voice she hardly recognized. It wasn't her stoic widow voice. It wasn't her quiet, *thank you so much for expressing your sympathies* tone. She sounded like a version of herself she'd forgotten existed. Carefree. Alive. Nothing like a ghost at all. "Are you here for the party?"

The cowboy's hard mouth shifted slightly, though Skylar would never call it a smile. He was too weathered and lethal for that, like a long, deadly pull of hundred-proof whiskey. And still, that little crook made Skylar flush.

Everywhere.

"I never turn down a lady's invitation to party," he told her, and his voice was like a lick, a faint rasp with too much electricity in its wake. "But I should warn you, I'm a bull rider. I like it hard and wild or not at all."

Skylar thought her mouth dropped open, even as heat roared through her, reminding her that whatever had happened these last, sad years, she was alive. Very much alive.

And the hottest cowboy she'd ever seen—certainly this close—was talking to her about sex. Not the kind of sex she was used to. But the kind that she'd only ever imagined when she was by herself.

He leveled a very male, very appraising look at her that

made her toes curl up in her sandals, and that crook in his mouth seemed to deepen. She felt as if he'd put his big, strong hands on her when he hadn't. When he didn't.

When she only wished he would.

But someone must have walked into the kitchen, because the noise of the party rushed into the house from behind her. The bull rider before her raised an eyebrow, a dare and a challenge or maybe just a simple command, and Skylar didn't think. She didn't know what to think.

She was tired of thinking.

He was the first man she'd so much as noticed since Thayer had died. And she wasn't thinking about Thayer at all, for once. Skylar didn't feel guilty about it—on the contrary, she felt as if, for the first time in forever, she wasn't a ghost.

This man didn't look through her. He didn't tell her he was sorry. He looked at her like he knew exactly what to do to make her scratch and scream like every wild story of a bad-to-the-bone bull rider she'd ever heard.

It made her feel alive again.

So Skylar just stepped back and let him in.

Chapter Two

CODY GALEN HATED promotional bullshit.

And pretty much everything else about this side of his bull-riding career, if he was honest, as he powered through what he was determined would be his last year on the circuit. But the promotional gambits were the worst.

Even at his most charming, Cody was not the kind of guy other men wanted to hang out and have a beer with. He wasn't easygoing. He'd never learned the intricacies of small talk and shooting the shit. Cody was more about hard whiskey than artisanal microbrews. He was the guy other men wanted at their back when the bar fight broke out, because he was afraid of nothing and impressed with even less than that, and it showed in every line of his body.

He might as well be a billboard for bad decisions with inevitably painful outcomes.

Which was the trouble with promo opportunities like this stupid sponsorship game he was playing today in Billings. Cody wasn't all that great at hiding the fact he'd rather be in a fistfight than at a picnic, and that made it tough to convince folks that he was the American Extreme

Bull Rider they wanted to splash their company names all over while he was out there pitting himself against the rankest bulls in existence and trying not to die.

The fact he tended to score high and win a lot had done his talking for him all these years, but Cody wasn't a young man anymore. He wasn't eighteen and cocky, unable to imagine any outcome but total domination. He'd broken just about every bone in his body more than once, torn ligaments and shoulders alike, suffered concussions and been rushed to hospitals all over the country and these days, his battered old body let him know it with every step. He was scarred and scuffed and nowhere near as shiny as he'd been back when.

Hell, his boots were shinier than he was.

You could try smiling, he reminded himself as he stood in the middle of a Fourth of July party in the crowded backyard of one Billy Grey, self-proclaimed sporting goods king of the west.

Maybe that wasn't fair. Maybe Grey Sports was bigger than Cody was giving it credit for. Lord knew it was the only thing that had impressed his mother in years. Meredith Devine didn't care that Cody was famous in some circles. She didn't care that he was the reason she got to keep living her sad little life in the South Dakota town where Cody had grown up, clinging on hard to the terrible marriage she still refused to leave.

Mama didn't mind spending his money, of course, but

she always acted like she didn't know how he'd come by it. Cody understood that, as far as he understood anything his mother did. He knew full well that if that asshole Todd, her husband for way too long now—and Cody refused to use the word *stepfather*—had to think too hard about how Cody's mom afforded their life outside of the money Todd drank away, it wouldn't end well for her.

That was something Meredith chose. Over and over again, no matter how many times and how many ways Cody had tried to save her. There was a point at which he had to stop giving a shit or lose his own, and he'd reached that point a long time ago. But his half-sisters were another matter. Kasey and Kathleen didn't deserve Todd as a father any more than Cody had deserved that punk as his only male authority figure after his own dad had died. Kasey and Kathleen had kept Cody in it, tethered to his mama's bad choices for the last twenty years no matter how much he wanted out.

His mother was real good at pretending. That she was happy. That she enjoyed the crappy little life she'd carved out with Todd after they'd lost Cody's father. She even pretended that she didn't know what was in the checks that Cody wrote her, every time he handed her one. But Grey Sports, for some reason, had made her light right up.

Who doesn't like Grey Sports? she'd asked, then pinched up her face as if she regretted showing that much emotion.

Last weekend the tour had been in Deadwood, which

meant there was no way for Cody to avoid a little family reunion, since he'd grown up within driving distance.

We wanted to come see you ride, his half-sister Kathleen had told him. In a whisper, behind her hand, because Kathleen was seventeen years old, almost free like her older sister, and knew better than to attract Todd's dark, seething attention. *We were rooting for you.*

Cody went out of his way to avoid South Dakota and his family as much as possible. His entire life, in fact, was carefully constructed to keep him as far away from his family as it was possible to get, something he was willing to throw money at when necessary, as long as it maintained that distance.

Hell, he rode bulls for a living. It was entirely possible that one of those glorious bastards might take him out one of these days, and if that kept his family away from him for good, he'd probably enjoy it.

That was why it was so strange that his mother had been impressed that he was going up early to Montana this week to make nice with Billy Grey ahead of the Billings rodeo. She'd not only heard of the chain of stores, she'd also heard of Billy Grey, personally.

He does those ads, she'd said, and had actually looked almost pretty again. The way she had when Cody had been a kid and his father was still alive.

Meredith acted like she'd never heard of Ty Murray, granddaddy of the PBR and one of Cody's personal heroes.

But she sure knew Billy Grey.

Because Billy Grey was exactly the kind of guy who other guys wanted to have a beer with, Cody saw as he watched the older man work his own party. He was charming. A salesman from head to toe. He lived in a nice house with a great view, up on a hill overlooking the town of Billings. He had a hot, young wife, and two little twin girls running around in case anyone doubted his virility. Cody knew the type.

And he also knew his job, for all that he was often a grumpy dick while doing it. This was his last year. He didn't think his body could take much more, and he didn't want to go out on a gurney. He'd told Meredith that last week, flatly, in case she'd missed it all the other times he'd said it.

I don't know why you keep telling me that like it's up to me what you do, his mother had said around her latest cigarette.

We don't need your charity, boy, Todd had chimed in, all bluster and bullshit, sitting in a house with no mortgage payment thanks to his stepson's charity.

Which Cody had ignored. Because this was it. His last tour. His last ride. And if he wasn't going out crippled, he wasn't going out on an assault charge either. No matter how much Todd deserved to get a beatdown at last.

And once he was no longer on the tour, who knew what the hell he'd do? Cody had no clue, because he hadn't thought beyond bull riding for years now. Whatever he did, he couldn't wait to do it far away from his mother and her bad choices, which he never planned to get close to again. In the meantime, he had to cozy up to salesmen like Billy, because he had two college educations to pay for.

When really, what he wanted to do was find the girl who'd answered the door and then disappeared.

It was dark by the time he managed it. The party was still going on in the light of about a million lanterns, plopped on tables and nestled in the grass. The nice thing about the dark was that it was harder for people to corner him, so Cody found himself on the outskirts of the big yard, where the manicured lawn gave way to a little bit of wilderness and the slope of a hill. Not real Montana wilderness, but the suggestion of it.

He figured the girl was long gone. She looked like picket white fences and photogenic babies in matching outfits, and that wasn't Cody. It never had been. He figured it never would be, because he was no good at the things women like that seemed to need. Like wanting that kind of quiet, settled life in the first place.

Or fidelity. Not that he'd ever tried.

He found her right about the time he'd given up on seeing her again, sitting there on an old picnic table more in the woods than out. She was sitting on the top of the table with her feet on the bench seat, holding a bottle of water between her palms.

And when she saw him come toward her out of the dark, she smiled.

There was no reason that should have rolled over Cody

the way it did, like she was something dangerous. Some kind of summer storm, just sitting there.

She was way too pretty. And prettier the longer he looked at her. She had dark brown hair cut into one of those sharp, layered looks that only seemed to draw his attention to the lushness of her mouth. Her smile was a little crooked, which sank through him like its own kind of heat. And her eyes were shadowed in the light of the flickering mosquito candle on the table beside her, but he knew they were blue. He remembered. Just like he remembered that they'd looked haunted when she opened the door, and then heated up in the next moment.

Oh yeah, he remembered entirely too many details about this one.

"You're missing the party," she said, in the same sweet voice she'd used before, with a hint of the South shading her words. "I'm pretty sure they're throwing it just for you."

"You got that backward. I'm the entertainment, that's all. I might as well be a clown."

She had a delicate little nose and she wrinkled it then. "Oh, I hope not. No one likes a clown. Not really."

Cody wasn't shy. He was used to the effect he had on women. And he knew this one wasn't his typical buckle bunny. For one thing, she wasn't trying to climb him like a tree. She was still sitting there, her dress pulled over her knees like she was demure. Ladylike, even, which wasn't a word he could remember using before about the women in his sphere. Or at all.

And he was enough of a bastard that all he wanted to do was mess her up.

Cody moved closer, until he was standing directly in front of her. He watched the way she flushed, red and hot, as if she had no control over herself. It made him even harder than he'd been when he'd spotted her sitting over here in the first place. Her blue eyes were wide and trained on his. That mouth of hers, temptingly crooked, was slightly open, as if she was having some trouble breathing. He aimed to make sure she did.

He reached over and settled his hand in the place where her neck met her shoulder, so he could feel her pulse go wild beneath his fingers.

"Holy shit," she whispered.

"Tell me what you want," he drawled, aware it was an order. And that he wasn't as relaxed about this as he usually was. But then, he was used to sure things. "Who knows? I might just grant your wish."

She blinked. "That's a complicated question."

"Darlin', it's only complicated if you make it complicated. My advice? Don't."

Her skin was so soft. This close, Cody could smell her shampoo, and a crisper scent he thought was soap. No perfume. No pretense. She wasn't even wearing too much makeup, just a little bit of mascara. She was fresh. Pretty in every sense of the term.

Definitely not for you, a sneering little voice inside of him chimed in. It sounded a hell of a lot like that douchebag Todd.

But all Cody wanted was a taste.

And he'd never paid much attention to Todd.

"Well," she said, drawing the word out. She tilted her head back a little, and that dazed look was fading. Replaced by something that made a dark, low fire kindle inside of him. Then begin to glow. "As it happens, I have quite a few wishes that need some granting."

"Hit me."

"I mean, you *are* a celebrity. This is like a grown-up Make-A-Wish situation, isn't it?"

"Very grown-up," he agreed, and saw her smile.

"My brother is getting married in a few weeks," she told him. "I really need a date. And I'd prefer that it was someone who didn't know anything about me. Interested?"

"I'm not good date material," Cody said, concentrating on the way her skin kept getting hotter and her pulse beat faster. "I have a tendency to horrify family members. My own as well as everyone else's. It's a gift."

"That would make you excellent date material for me," she said, but there was nothing particularly serious in her voice. Maybe that was why he hadn't already walked away. "My family could use a little horrifying."

Then she laughed. And there was something about the way she did it. As if she hadn't done it in a long time. As if the laugh itself was rusty, and surprised her, somehow.

Cody had no idea why the sound of it seemed to hang there inside of him, then grow. As if her laughter was taking hold of him, gripping him, changing him—

But that was ridiculous.

And he didn't know what was going on with this girl. He didn't know why he'd walked out of a party filled with other, far easier women to find this one sitting by herself in the dark. That wasn't how he normally rolled. Cody liked it easy. He was a hard man by trade and inclination, with coal where his heart should have been according to entirely too many wannabe exes, and he was a little too calm about the fact he spent most of his days *this close* to his own death.

When it came to women, he never had to work too hard. He liked party girls and they really, *really* liked him. And bull riders got through the demands of their lives in two ways. They were either drunk on Jesus, or they were drunk, full stop. The godly folks tended to come with wives and kids, giving them that much more to pray for. Cody, meanwhile, came with a whiskey bottle. He was always up for a good time and he liked the girls who wanted to give him one. Buckle bunnies who knew their place. Here today, gone tomorrow, and maybe, just maybe, back for a second round next year when the tour rolled through again.

No drama. No haunted eyes, for Christ's sake. No sitting all alone on the edge of a big party, clearly with way too much going on for a man like him, who opted not to care about anything. Especially not dates to weddings.

"Let me guess," he said, and he should have moved away from her, but he didn't. He kept his hand where it was, then let his thumb stroke its way back and forth along the line of her throat. He felt the shudder she tried to repress, rolling through her like a quiet sort of thunder, the hint of another storm. And he couldn't have said how exactly he moved even closer, until his hips were almost between her knees. "You're a good girl."

There was a hint of that crooked smile. And a hint of that haunting, besides. But if there was extra emotion in the blue sheen of her eyes, it didn't seem to bother her. So Cody told himself it didn't bother him.

"The best," she whispered. "I'm practically a saint."

"Nothing I like better than desecrating something holy, darlin'."

He felt the way her heart jumped at that. The way her pulse kicked into a higher gear. He expected her to pull away, but she didn't.

She didn't.

"I was hoping you'd say something like that," she murmured instead.

Cody held her gaze. He reached up and took his hat from his head, and set it down on the table. He put his finger and thumb against his mouth, wetting them. Then he reached out to the little bucket candle beside her, and extinguished the flame. With a pinch.

Leaving the two of them alone in the dark, no flickering light to give them away.

Then Cody indulged himself and did exactly what he'd wanted to do since the moment he'd found her over here. Hidden just inside the tree line, with the party a good distance below them. It was a perfect spot, really, for all kinds of things the good folks of Billings, Montana, wouldn't want to look at directly.

He told himself that was why he was so interested in her. Because she seemed a little complicated on the surface, sure, but she'd set this whole thing up beautifully. Because she was making it so easy it was like she was just another girl in a bar, easily digested and forgotten.

Because she aimed that crooked smile at him and it made him crazy.

Cody moved so he was between her knees. Then he picked her up with an arm around her, shifting her as he moved forward so he could lay her flat on the tabletop. Then he followed her right down, settling himself between her thighs, snug up against her, as if the table had been made to hold them just like this.

Her breath went out in a shudder that was half a laugh. He could hear her nerves, and he shouldn't have liked that. It told him she wasn't like his usual girls who did this sort of thing all the time.

Maybe he was tired of *usual.* It'd been the same old, same old for so long now, Cody only knew where he was when they yelled out the name of the city as he walked into one dusty arena after the next. He only knew who he was with his hand roped tight against a bull's back. The mighty animal beneath him, more powerful than he could ever dream of being, made his head go clear. Calm.

As if the only thing in the world that could ever matter were those eight sweet seconds he needed to score. The most dangerous dance on earth.

But maybe she was the next best thing, something inside him whispered. Because stretched out over her, here in the dark, he felt that same intense calm creep over him. Settling him.

She didn't push him off. Or giggle in that cloying way he usually had to block out with the girls who chased him around because of what he could do on a bull. He could feel her shivering slightly, as if she was having trouble controlling her own excitement. Or nerves.

She shifted a little below him, but it was only to accommodate him more. And she was so soft. Her thighs gripped him, and he wished he wasn't wearing jeans.

But he could feel her breasts, sweet little curves pressed tight against his chest. And he could feel the way her arms came up to hold on to his waist with a surprisingly hard grip.

And it wasn't so dark that he couldn't see her face, even prettier up close.

Everything about her was pretty. It kept catching at him, like one of these times it might stick.

"You got here fast," she said, laughter in her voice and something he couldn't read in her gaze. He concentrated on the heat. "You could give a girl whiplash."

"I'm a bull rider, baby," he drawled, and he nearly smiled as he said it. "You'd be amazed what I can accomplish in a few good seconds."

She laughed again. He didn't know what it was about that laugh. It was so different from the calculated giggling he knew too well from all those bars, from across pool tables and huddled in dark corners. It was an entirely different animal, light and tempting.

It did things to him he didn't understand.

So he ignored it. He concentrated on what he knew. The same way he did when the gate opened and there was nothing but him and the bull leaping and rolling and bucking beneath him. He concentrated on the dance of it, not the deeper things he didn't want to acknowledge in the moment.

The heat in her gaze, not the haunted part.

The way she gripped him, not the way she laughed.

The fact he wanted her, hard and wild, as if he'd been wanting her for a long, long time. When the truth was, he didn't even know her name.

He told himself that was a good thing. Names were intimate. Names...meant things.

He didn't want to know her name. He didn't want to *mean* anything. He just wanted her, that was all.

Cody bent his head down, taking her mouth at last, and he made that matter.

Because it was the only thing that ever could.

Chapter Three

OBVIOUSLY SKYLAR KNEW better.

But her cowboy was kissing her, and she found she didn't care too much about what she knew.

She cared a whole lot more about how she felt.

Because this was clearly insanity, and yet he tasted so good she thought that all this time she'd been getting it wrong. She'd wanted so badly to be normal again. To blend in instead of stand out. To be just like everyone else and no kind of shrine at all, when really, what she'd wanted was this.

This. Him.

It was like fireworks—

But no, she told herself as sensation swamped her. It was the Fourth of July. If there were fireworks, it was to celebrate the holiday. *He* wasn't doing it, no matter how she felt inside.

Still, she didn't check the dark night sky somewhere above them. She let all that pop and sizzle and crash happen inside her no matter what might or might not be happening above them.

Because all Skylar could concentrate on was him.

He was harder, more solid and more muscled, than he appeared at first sight—and at first sight she'd thought he was pure granite in jeans and cowboy boots. He'd looked lanky despite that, standing out there on her father's step, but it turned out that every part of him was built tough. Like weathered steel, everywhere.

And she could feel him everywhere, because he was so big and so hard, impossibly hot to the touch, and *on top* of her.

She had no idea where the hem of her dress had ridden up to and she couldn't say she cared. She let her hands move along his sides, feeling his heat and strength through his shirt. He was too warm, too hot, and the coolness of the summer evening now that it was dark didn't seem to make a difference. He generated a heat all his own.

In some distant part of her brain, Skylar knew that there would be entirely too much to think about when this was over. She'd never been this girl. She'd never done anything like this before. She'd only ever touched one man this way, and she'd intended to marry him. She'd always been a little bit old-fashioned. That was what happened when your mother was a monument to romantic bitterness and your father remarried like it was his job. It had always made sense to Skylar to take it slow. To make sure.

And look what that got you, a bitter voice inside her sang out.

She shoved it aside. Because the truth was, if this was out

of character, she liked it. She encouraged it. Because whatever character she'd had, whatever person she'd been before, that Skylar had been lost two years ago.

That Skylar was dead.

And that was okay. Because the Skylar who was stretched out on the old picnic table, way out in the furthest shadows of the backyard with a cowboy pressed against her in the dark, didn't care who she'd been. The Skylar who met his hard, demanding mouth with her own wanted one thing. One thing only.

More.

So she angled her mouth to get a better fit and she pressed herself against him, wrapping her arms around his waist and hooking her legs over his.

Everything seemed to burst into flame then. All at once.

Her cowboy laughed a little bit, right against her mouth. He shifted slightly, moving one of his hands to her propped-up leg. He smoothed it over her knee, his hand hard and calloused, then found her thigh. And he laughed again when she hissed something that wasn't quite a word as she tipped her head back against the table and surrendered herself to the storm of his touch, charging through her, lighting her up.

He didn't hesitate. At all. She didn't know why that made everything that much hotter.

It was as if he knew. As if he'd known from the moment she'd opened the front door that it would be like this. That he would be sprawled over her in the dark, about to discover that she was hot and wet in a great many ways she didn't know how to explain. Or express.

The cute little boy shorts she wore as underwear hardly deterred him. He slid his hand beneath them, making a low, very male noise of appreciation when he found her.

"So wet," he muttered.

That didn't seem like something that needed commentary, and that was a good thing, because Skylar could hardly breathe. His hand was so big. Hard and faintly rough. She could feel the slight, delicious abrasion as he caressed her, moving through her folds, then finding the neediest part of her that easily.

As if he'd known that too. Exactly how it would be.

She sucked in a breath—to say something maybe, or cry out, or who even knew—but he was already thrusting his fingers inside of her. And he dragged his thumb against her clit as he did it.

Again. And again.

Until Skylar couldn't pretend that she was capable of thought. She was nothing but wild, humming, spinning sensation. She arched up against him, rocking herself against his talented, clever hand, because in that instant she would do anything for this. For him.

For a hard, unsmiling man who looked at her as if she was nothing more than a particularly hot piece of ass, and then proved it.

It was liberating.

More than that, it was so damn good.

"Concentrate, baby," he muttered against her neck, and then he twisted his fingers and surged in deep.

Skylar broke apart. She screamed, maybe, and she didn't care who heard it. And it was only when she'd shuddered and shuddered, shaking so hard that moisture leaked out of her eyes and she thought she might not stop, that she came back down and realized she was still spread out on that picnic table.

And he still had his fingers deep inside of her, but his free hand curled over her lips to keep the noise inside.

That mouth of his still didn't smile. But those eyes that she knew were a mysterious green danced.

"You're welcome." He sounded full of himself, arrogant and male, and better than anything Skylar could remember hearing. Ever. "I kept you from screaming so loud you brought everyone in that party running up here to see what was wrong."

He lifted his palm from her mouth, and she could taste him. Hot. Hard. Faintly rough.

Perfect.

"Thank you," she managed to say primly in a voice that was much too scratchy to be hers. "I'm not sure I care."

"I'll keep that in mind," her cowboy murmured, more laughter in his voice if still not on his face. She had no idea why that made her chest feel almost too tight to bear. But then it was impossible to care, because he was pulling his fingers from the deep clench of her pussy. And it made her shudder all over again. "You going to come again?"

Skylar smiled. "That seems greedy."

"Greed is good." He gathered her closer to him, then rolled until she was splayed out on top of him. "I heard it in a movie, so it must be true."

"That sounds reasonable to me," she whispered.

He reached up one of those hands, so masterful and strong it made her stomach flip over, hooked it around her neck, and tugged her mouth down to his.

And for a long time, she was simply lost in that. In him. The sensation still storming around and around inside of her, telling her in no uncertain terms that she was alive.

Gloriously, beautifully alive.

She had his shirt pulled out of his waistband and her hands beneath it, all over that chiseled steel chest of his. She rocked herself against the hard ridge of his jeans below her, making both of them groan. And still he kissed her, a fierce and wild sort of taking, teeth and lips and desperation.

Skylar had never felt anything like this in her life.

And then he was moving again. His strength was almost impossible, she thought in a daze. He picked her up as if she weighed nothing at all. Then he sat up on the top of the table, and swung around to the side, so she was splayed out over his lap.

Then he reached down between them, unbuckled his belt, took his sweet time pulling down his zipper, and then finally, finally pulled his cock free.

She thought maybe she died in the time it took. Died and came back and died again, so greedy was she for this. All of this. She wanted to glut herself on every last bit of sensation.

Skylar didn't play around now, pretending to be shy. She reached down and wrapped her hands around him, loving the little sound he made when she did. The little hiss of breath that told her that no matter how controlled he was, she got to him too.

It thrilled her.

She stacked her hands, one on top of the other, and then moved them. Slowly and luxuriously. Up and down.

Once. Twice.

"Enough." His voice was different now. Strained. Dark.

As if he was as greedy as she was.

More, maybe.

Skylar felt his big hands move between them again. He dealt with the condom and then she felt a few sharp tugs. It took her a minute to realize he was ripping her underwear off of her as she sat there, her legs open over his lap.

And there was something so animalistic about it. So greedy and delirious. She nearly came again, just from that.

And then he was lifting her, tipping her toward him and holding her where he wanted her, so that the broad head of his cock was moving through her folds. Nudging against her clit to send wild sparks showering through her, then back through her wet pussy as if he was situating himself—

Except he clearly knew what he was doing.

It dawned on Skylar that he was playing with her.

Her heart kicked at her, and then slowly, so slowly, as if he had all night and could take all the time he liked, he started to work himself inside of her.

"So fucking tight," he muttered.

"I can't tell if that's a compliment," she whispered in return, half laughing.

"It's a goddamn song of joy."

It felt like joy. He did. And he kept going, deeper and deeper.

Like every other part of him, his cock was like steel. And much bigger than she'd expected. He was splitting her open. He was filling her, hard and deep. He was making her new.

And when he was finally all the way inside of her, stretching her to the hilt, he wrapped his hands around her hips and opened his strong thighs beneath her.

Skylar pulled in a breath. Because she was ready. More than ready. As if all this heat and all this fire—all the wild, intense sensation, melting and raging inside of her—was the change she'd always needed.

Two years later, she was finally dealing with the things that therapy and time could not.

"Skylar?"

Skylar froze. Below her and inside her, her cowboy shifted, his gaze moving over her face as if he was trying to read her.

"Skylar? Are you there?"

It was Angelique. A woman who was all of eighteen months older than Skylar, and yet also her stepmother, which never got less awkward. Skylar had no idea why she was looking for her—

Well, that wasn't entirely true. She and Angelique were friendly. More friendly than Skylar had ever imagined they would be, back when Jesse had refused to acknowledge her and Skylar had tried her best to stay polite, but distant.

But this wasn't really the time to think about her relationship with her stepmother.

"Maybe she heard you," her cowboy said, his voice barely more than a whisper and much too close to her ear, sending a shivery thing dancing down her spine to pool there where their bodies were connected.

Skylar didn't twist around to look, but she knew that Angelique must have been standing on the lawn. Peering out into the darker woods.

"She can't actually see me, can she?" Skylar asked, her voice shallow and soft.

"Let's hope not," her cowboy murmured.

But he didn't really sound like he'd care too much either way.

Something that Skylar shouldn't have found the least bit hot. And yet.

He pulled out then, making Skylar bite her lip and let

out a tiny little sound of protest, but then everything was spinning. It took her a minute to realize that she was. Literally.

He lifted her up and spun her around, and then settled her on his lap again. But this time, she was facing the party down below. She could see all the lights and people milling about, and a shadow on the edge of everything that she could tell was her stepmother.

And she didn't care about any of it, because her cowboy was working her down onto his cock again, every ridiculously hard inch of him making her want to scream.

It was that good. It was fire and heat and perfection.

But this time, she didn't have his hand over her mouth to keep her quiet. This time, she had to do it herself.

And the fact that she wasn't sure if she could or not, when she could see Angelique's silhouette right there in front of her, should have terrified her. She wished she was drunk. That would be some kind of excuse.

But in the next breath, she decided she didn't need any excuse.

She didn't understand why sex with a stranger should affect her like this. *How* it could. The impression she'd gotten from her more adventurous friends over the years was that this wasn't how it normally went. But then again, they were usually too drunk to know better.

Or so they'd always claimed. As if maybe the sex would have been amazing if they could remember it clearly.

Skylar wasn't drunk. She was stone-cold sober, and for the first time in two years, was doing something that had nothing at all to do with grief.

If anything, it felt like flying.

And then he began to move.

Slow. Hot. Deliberate.

"Skylar? Are you up there?" Angelique called out again, and Skylar shuddered. The man behind her only let out a sound that was slightly too gravelly to be a laugh, and then pressed his mouth into the crook of her neck.

"I thought I saw her go up there," Angelique was saying to whoever was standing with her. "Maybe she went back into the house."

The cowboy kept moving. Long and deep. Inexorable. And Skylar was reborn. Remade.

From one thrust to the next, she was undone. Made new.

He held her with his hard steel band of an arm around her waist, his mouth at her neck, and that other hand of his sneaking down to the place where they were joined, to roll her clit between his fingers as he slammed himself into her.

It was hard. It was intense. It was dirty—and it was glorious.

She fell apart once, in a wild sort of shudder she thought should have shattered her into actual pieces, but he didn't stop. He didn't even pause, as if he knew her body would hum from one intense peak straight into the next, and as if he didn't much care if she caught her breath or not.

It was too intense and then it was wild again, one stroke to the next, and he kept right on going. He built her up again, threw her over that cliff again, and still he kept going.

Once. Twice. Then once again.

And only when she was limp against him, holding her own hands to her mouth to keep the sounds she made inside, biting on her own fingers to stay silent, did he finally let himself go.

He threw Skylar over one last time as he went himself, while fireworks burst open in the sky above them as if he'd made them, too. As if he'd ripped open the sky and filled it with all the color and light he'd poured into her.

And for a while, they just sat there. Skylar was limp in his lap, collapsed against his chest. She tried her best to breathe, but couldn't say she cared all that much if she did or didn't. Not when she couldn't feel her fingers.

He recovered faster, which didn't surprise Skylar at all. She didn't object when he picked her up again, pulling out of her as he lifted her, then setting her beside him on the picnic table as if she was made of glass. But a different kind of glass. The kind he expected could survive a hurricane or two, if she had to guess. Not the shattering, delicate, fragile kind.

Not the glass she'd been for years that everyone tiptoed around, so fearful of another crack.

She breathed in, then out. She willed her heart to slow back down. She willed her breath to stop catching in her throat.

And Skylar had no experience with this. She didn't know what was supposed to happen in the cool dark of a Montana summer night between two people who had never so much as introduced themselves. She imagined doing that now. Putting on a carefree smile and acting like all those girls she'd envied a little, back when she was younger. When some part of her had worried she was missing out.

But she felt something shift inside of her, as if in warning. And she didn't want to try to play any games when she didn't know the rules. She didn't want to get to know the man when the cowboy had taken her on a much-needed holiday from herself and her legacy and her whole, tortured story.

There was a whole party down there filled with people who would tell her how sorry they were. They would make concerned faces the moment they saw her and ask her how she was in low, intense tones. But not this man. He'd wanted her, so he'd taken her. He had no idea who she was. And somehow, he'd set something free inside of her. Shifted that great, squatting weight of grief over an inch or two to let a little light in.

Skylar needed to protect it, whatever it was.

And she certainly couldn't do that, she realized then, if she sat around having a strained, awkward conversation with this man about…whatever it was people talked about when they just up and had sex while they were still strangers.

Skylar didn't know the protocols. She didn't know how people navigated things like this when everyone's clothes were back on and real life was closing in again.

But that was the beauty of having lost everything. It meant she literally had nothing left to lose. She remembered how worried she'd been, way back when she'd started dating Thayer. About everything. What to wear, what to say, whether he liked her, whether he'd call…

She didn't care about any of that now. She wasn't sure she ever would again. She'd learned a terrible lesson in what was really important, and there was no stitching herself back together to be the heedless girl she'd once been.

So while he worked on his buckle, Skylar simply stood up. She reached down to find her tattered, ripped panties on the ground, balled them up, and stuck them into the pocket of her sundress. She smoothed down the skirt, and then she reached up and did the same to her hair, the comfortable gesture soothing her.

"Thank you," she said. Formally.

Too formally, she realized the next instant, when his head tilted slightly to one side and that hard gaze of his settled on her.

"Thank you?" he repeated.

Which told her that was clearly the wrong thing to say.

But Skylar didn't need to say anything more than that. She knew he was a bull rider. She could probably find out who he was in an instant, with a simple Google search, if she wanted. She didn't want. Not tonight. There were fireworks up ahead, and still entirely too many inside of her, and she was content.

Changed.

Free of chains she hadn't even known were holding her back.

"Thank you," she said again, firmly.

And then she turned away, and headed back down toward the house. Leaving her cowboy and the things they'd done together behind her in the dark. Because up ahead of her was light, and she was finally ready to embrace it.

She was finally ready to let it shine on her.

Chapter Four

THE LOCAL SPONSORS' COCKTAIL event was in full swing the Thursday night before the weekend bull-riding event and Skylar's cheeks ached a little with all the polite smiling she was called upon to do as a representative of Grey Sports. Not to mention the laughing without finding anything all that funny, necessarily, or the pretending to understand what overly boisterous men with their too-red noses shouted at her over the clamor.

You were an event planner for how many years? her father had asked when she'd suggested that she might not be the best choice for the job. Especially given the fact her step-mother was a former model and could always just stand somewhere and stun men to grateful, exuberant silence. *You can work a room like your old man, Skylar. It's a gift.*

Skylar wasn't sure it was a gift she wanted, but that was what she was here for tonight, so she did her best to make each smile seem as genuine as possible. She used all the tricks she'd learned at the events planning firm she'd interned at after college and had worked in ever since, right up until she'd left Atlanta.

Even when the people she was smiling at were old family friends who knew all about her and her last few years, which meant a whole lot of apologetic glances and the odd squeeze of her arm instead of easy cocktail conversation. That was when all those friendly smiles and easy pivots in conversation served her well, and an event like this was simple in that regard, because everyone in the room was a fan of the American Extreme Bull Riders Tour and more than happy to discuss it. At length.

Every conversation she was a part of turned to statistics and rankings—either on its own or because Skylar made sure of it. This bull. That rider. What had happened last weekend in Deadwood, South Dakota, who people thought would claim the top spot in Billings this Saturday night, and their take on the season so far for the tough, athletic cowboys who fought to score high and keep riding, week after week, despite injuries and uncooperative bulls and whatever else might befall them along the way.

She did not think about the man she'd left behind her in the dark. She didn't think about the long, hot shower she'd taken when she'd gone into the house that night, when every square inch of her skin had seemed *alive* with sensation and the hot water had only exacerbated it. She certainly didn't think of all the dark, erotic images that had chased through her head as she'd tried to will herself to sleep. They'd followed her into her dreams and yet, despite that, she'd slept deeper and woke more refreshed than she had in ages.

She told herself *that* was because she'd had sex again, pure and simple. It was because of all that release, that was all. A physical reaction to all those endorphins—nothing more and nothing less and certainly nothing to worry about.

Or hate herself for in the bright, unsparing glare of the morning after, tucked up in her childhood bedroom with no shadows to hide in.

"Simple biology," she'd muttered to herself as she'd gotten dressed, entirely too aware of how different her body felt. A twinge here, a faint scrape there. That tugging, low in her belly, as if her cowboy had woken up something deep within her and it wasn't going back to sleep.

And more than that, the odd sensation that she was turned inside out, somehow, though she looked the same on the outside. That she'd crossed a line she didn't entirely understand and there was no going back now. No changing what would happen next—what she'd put into motion with that recklessness she hadn't known was in her.

She refused to feel badly about it.

Skylar had stood in a pool of sunlight in her bedroom and breathed in, past that odd little uncertain feeling that she suspected wanted to bloom into shame, and then blew it all out.

She would not feel badly about doing something she'd wanted to do, and so well, apparently, that she was still flying high all those hours later. *She would not.*

Thayer had been dead for years. It was long past time

Skylar set about crawling out of his grave. And there was nothing to feel badly about in any of that.

Even if she was starting to suspect that she'd viewed herself as a shrine to Thayer all this time, maybe even more than others did.

Angelique had blinked at her across the kitchen island downstairs a little while later and asked her why she was in such a good mood all of a sudden, and Skylar had tried to dim the silly smile she hadn't realized she'd been aiming at her coffee. She'd chalked it up to an unexpectedly good night's sleep. That was what she'd told her stepmother.

But the good mood had lasted. All of yesterday and into today. She'd gotten ready for the party this evening with a little too much anticipation bubbling around inside of her, fizzy and impossible.

She didn't know her cowboy's name and she'd gone out of her way to make sure she didn't learn it. That was how she wanted it, because what mattered was that she'd felt something again. She'd *felt.*

It was her gift to herself. The other night could fade into memory, as darkly erotic as the images in her head, and there would never be any need to deal with what she'd done in reality.

Skylar was full up on reality.

But she'd always loved the rodeo. Bull fighting and barrel racing, roping and all the rest of it. She'd had the odd dream of being a bit of a cowgirl in her time, like every other girl growing up in Montana and the rest of rural America, but it had never taken. She hadn't gone on to dedicate her life to horses, ranching, or farming the way so many of her high school classmates had. Most of the time, she didn't have any regrets about that. Of course, most of the time, she also wasn't back home in Billings, her life at a serious crossroads.

This weekend was as close as she'd get to the childhood dreams of land and the West and the particular sweetness of Montana that she only ever seemed to have when she came back here, and she was resolved to enjoy it. She would talk stock and stats and get her western cowgirl on tonight. She would work at her father's booth in the Rimrock Auto Arena this weekend while the bull riders did their thing.

She would be grateful for her own very personal Independence Day the other night, and on Monday she could figure out what on earth she was going to do with this brand-new life of hers.

It wasn't the one she'd planned, but it was still hers. Like it or not.

Skylar was determined that she would live it. No matter what that looked like.

"Here you are," she heard her father's familiar voice boom from behind her then, jolting her back from that little spiral off into the ether. She'd moved off to the far side of the party for a little breather by the restaurant's big windows, but she was sure the few moments she'd had were enough. She was already smiling when his arm landed on her shoulders and swung her a good one-eighty around from where she'd been standing, looking out at the summer evening hanging on over downtown Billings, gold and blue and breathless. "I want you to meet someone, sweetheart."

And Skylar had spent years learning her party smile, which was much different from her widow's smile. Polite and even a little merry, as befit a party. Delighted straight through, from her eyelashes to her dimples. Her old boss had claimed that a woman's greatest power lay in how well she mastered, harnessed, and deployed her smile.

But when Skylar saw the man standing there with her father, dark eyes glittering and no trace of a smile on his hard mouth, her stomach seemed to free-fall straight out of her body and through the floor beneath her feet.

Because it was him, of course. Her cowboy.

The last man on earth she wanted to see again.

Though her body hadn't gotten that message. Her heart was thumping at her. Her pulse was so loud in her ears that for a moment she worried she might have gone deaf. And everything else was a riot.

She concentrated on holding herself very, very still, as if the slightest movement would give her away.

Her cowboy didn't look a whole lot different than he had the other night, though he'd foregone his hat this time, which only called more attention to the careless way he wore his dark-blond hair. He wore a different button-down shirt, a bit fancier and with a hint of western flair, that only seemed to emphasize those strong shoulders of his and his narrow hips. Skylar could see the shiny, obviously handcrafted belt buckle he wore that announced his prowess at his sport, and then she jerked her eyes back up because she didn't need to look below his waist. She already knew what he had in his jeans.

And that gleam in his eyes told her he remembered it all just as clearly as she did.

"This is my oldest daughter, Skylar," her father was saying in that hearty salesman's voice of his that usually made her brother roll his eyes, but had always made Skylar feel loved. Protected. Home, even.

She felt none of those things tonight. Not even close.

The cowboy's hard green gaze moved all over her, relentless and entirely too knowing. She had no doubt that he could see the way she flushed, almost instantaneously, as if the way their gazes clung together for that brief, hot, stomach-dropping first second of recognition was his mouth on her body.

Skylar was certain he suspected—or just knew—that the rest of her was mounting a revolution against the calm exterior she was working hard to keep in place. She felt like a knot, inside and out. She felt slippery between her legs, melting and aching and needy. All over again. And she was terrified that if she looked down, she would see her own nipples, hard and obvious behind the thin fabric of the dress she wore.

She didn't look down.

The cowboy's hard mouth was in a flat line, and the fact she knew how he tasted was no reason she should feel…deliciously hollow. Scraped raw.

Hot and shuddery, and something like greedy, all the way through.

And they were standing there with her father. *Her father.* It was so horrifying that Skylar almost burst into a spate of completely inappropriate laughter. Because she could hardly think what other reaction she ought to have in a situation like this, besides tears.

Her father was still talking, and Skylar hadn't heard a single word he said. Was he telling this man she couldn't really claim was a stranger her tragic life story? She couldn't hear over the racket her pulse was making. But there was no hint of sympathy or softness or the typical uneasiness on the cowboy's face, so she doubted it.

Skylar could feel something a little too close to hysteria clawing at the back of her throat, and promised herself that whatever else happened, she would not open her mouth and make it worse. For example, she absolutely would not say: *Oh, Dad, you don't need to introduce us. I can't say I know his name, but I did get acquainted with far more important parts of him in the dark on the picnic table up behind the house.*

Billy Grey might not have led much by example when it came to morality, with all his affairs and wives, but that didn't make him any less her father. In the sense that he certainly wouldn't want to hear about the sexual exploits of his little girl and would likely react to tales of such things badly. Very, very badly.

Skylar felt caught in a harsh grip, as if the cowboy had his hands wrapped around her throat. Or that hard arm of his that he used to keep himself situated on the back of a twelve-hundred-pound bull tight around her middle again.

She couldn't breathe. She didn't want to breathe.

What she ought to do, she understood in a flash, was simply turn and get away from this. From him. Run, if necessary. Do whatever she had to do to put space between her and this man of granite who stared at her as if he planned to take her apart.

Piece by piece, with no thought or expectation of ever putting her back together again.

Possibly right here and now.

But her father was still talking in his merry way, completely oblivious to the tension swirling around him.

"This right here is Cody Galen," he said, sounding genuinely thrilled that he had the opportunity to introduce Skylar to such a star. And *star* was the right word. Skylar didn't follow bull riding that closely but she'd heard his name before. "One of the American Extreme Bull Riders Tour veterans, and for my money, one of the best damn bull riders ever."

Cody, Skylar thought, unable to help herself. His name was Cody.

Her first thought was that it wasn't a hard enough name for a man who made steel look weak in comparison. But then her gaze drifted down the length of his hard, lean chest again, back to that belt buckle. It shone bright like the trophy it was, no doubt won on the back of an absolute monster of a bull somewhere, with all the broken bones and pulled muscles and torn ligaments that went with it. Weeks on the road and an endless season and injuries that would sideline most athletes, all for eight perfect seconds in one arena or the next. And *Cody* suited him, she thought. It was an unflinching western name. It sounded like the cowboy he was.

And she knew *Cody Galen,* who she'd heard about for years in the same distant way she knew about all the greats of the sports events she didn't watch, was one of the best.

That his name rang through her like some kind of bell, she would keep to herself. As if it was the answer to a question, when she knew it wasn't. Because he wasn't, either. He was just a man. Just a cowboy.

Just a one-night fling, and that night was over.

"I'm afraid my daughter doesn't follow bull riding as closely as her daddy does," her father was saying now, apparently unaware of the way the cowboy next to him was watching the daughter in question with a look that Skylar could only call predatory. She had to fight to repress her shiver—but she would have sworn Cody saw it anyway.

"They can't all be cowgirls," he drawled.

Her father laughed. Skylar realized her smile was slipping off her own mouth, and that would call even more attention to what was happening. More than that, it would show Cody that she wasn't handling this well. And she wanted—she *needed*—to handle this well. She wanted to laugh it all off. She wanted to play that light and airy, carefree girl she was certain someone else would be in a situation like this, but the truth was, she didn't know if she had that in her.

"It's an honor to meet you," she said instead, summoning up every bit of professional polish she'd learned at her old job, and beaming at Cody as she said it. "My father really is a huge fan."

There was the faintest hint of a curve on that granite mouth of his, then. Maybe that was what pricked at her. Skylar didn't know what devil it was, but she suddenly stopped caring that she was flushed too hot. She had no reason to be embarrassed. It wasn't as if he knew any more about her than she did about him. So she allowed her gaze to get a little challenging as she held his, watched the answering flare in his dark green eyes, and then stuck out her hand as if they'd really never met before.

As if she was going to pretend they never had.

And when Cody reached out to take it in the next instant, because every cowboy had manners, at least in public, she didn't look away. She didn't react to the shower of sparks that seemed to course over her when his hand closed around hers. She even pretended she couldn't feel that punch of sensation low in her belly.

No ache, she told herself. No deep melting.

It was just a handshake like all the others she'd had tonight. Impersonal gestures that made people feel as if they were connecting without having to actually do so.

"The pleasure's all mine, ma'am," Cody said after a moment, and Skylar didn't really understand how the man's drawl could get even slower. Until it rivaled molasses.

Or maybe that was just how it felt sliding over her, into her, until she wanted nothing more than to tear her hand out of his. And then stop whatever game she thought she was playing with this man who was so obviously used to various debaucheries that nights like the one they'd had were run of the mill to him, and hightail it out of this restaurant.

And maybe out of Billings, for that matter.

Instead, she let him hold her hand for a shade too long. Then she waited until he was the one to drop it, and found that she was inordinately proud of herself for something that she couldn't even call a victory. Especially not when his dark green eyes were gleaming at her, showing a kind of very male amusement that had even made it down to that distracting curve in the corner of his mouth.

And Skylar didn't run. She stood there instead, as if she was hanging on every word her father was saying when the truth was, she doubted she'd be able to repeat a single syllable of it later if her life depended on it.

Inside, she was still spinning. Reeling, if she was honest.

And she didn't want that. She'd hoped she wouldn't see Cody again. But now that she had, there was no need to make it dramatic. There was nothing dramatic about it, surely.

When another local vendor called out to her father and he started to move away, Skylar smiled politely and tried to go with him.

But everything in her went still when she felt a big, calloused hand wrap around her wrist and hold her tight.

"I'm not as familiar with Billings as I'd like to be," Cody said, in the most amiable, genial voice she'd heard from him yet. It was so out of character that she actually did a double take, and was sure that was a smile there on his arrogant mouth. "I'd sure appreciate it if a local could give me a few recommendations."

"Skylar would be happy to do that," her father said at once, because she probably would have been if it had been anyone else asking. "She might even give you a tour, if you ask nicely."

"I'm not much of a tour guide," Skylar demurred at once.

"You haven't let me ask you," Cody replied. "Nicely."

And somehow her father managed not to hear the sensual menace in the way he said it. But Skylar certainly did. Still, there was nothing to do but stand there, a smile pasted to her face despite how sharp it felt, while Billy walked off and left her there in Cody's clutches.

Literally.

She took her time looking back at him and told herself she was just gathering her strength and preparing to be easy. Carefree. Unbothered, the way she wanted to be. But the truth was, everything felt intimate again—and had since she'd locked eyes with him. There was a crowd all around them, just as there had been the other night. She knew people could see them, which made this much more public and safe than the other night at her father's house.

It shouldn't have felt dangerous. But oh, how it did.

Skylar made herself face him fully, because she didn't want to. She refused to be a coward.

"I don't know how this works," she told him before he could say a word. She even kept her smile on her face. "But if you think this is an opportunity to let me down easy, or condescend to me, or make me feel bad about what happened that night, you can just let go of my arm and let me walk away right now."

Skylar pulled against his grip, but he didn't loosen it. Of course he didn't. This was a man who held on tight while a deadly bull bucked him back and forth—what made her think she could pry his hand open if he didn't want to open it?

She frowned at him, forgetting about the pleasant expression she wanted to wear. "I'm not kidding."

"Exactly what do you think I'm going to say to you?" he asked, and his voice had gone all…lazy.

That was worse than the molasses before. It dripped all over her, hot and sweet. And hot in ways she didn't know how to handle.

"I don't know. That's the problem. I suppose you could say anything. I'm sure you do these things all the time."

Skylar didn't know why his gaze changed a little at that. It got more intent. Hotter, somehow. It made her want to squirm in her sandals.

"Darlin'," he said, and she knew she shouldn't like the way he said that. Especially when she was sure a man like him used it so he wouldn't have to concern himself with remembering names. "What benefit would there possibly be to me making you feel bad?"

As he spoke, he let his thumb move up and down along the inside of her wrist. An easy, almost offhanded little caress, so light it could have been an accident.

It wasn't an accident.

An accident wouldn't have felt like an avalanche. It wouldn't have roared through her, making her nipples pull tight and her belly go taut, while her pussy was so slippery and so wildly hot she was half afraid that it was visible from across the room.

Or even just to him.

Skylar pulled in a breath and it shook. Audibly. And that dark green gaze Cody kept trained on her got that much more intent.

So intent that something in her…shifted. As if a knot

suddenly pulled free.

"My understanding is that it's not a one-night stand unless both parties show some measure of shame about the experience," she heard herself say then, as if she was someone else. Someone who tilted her head to look up at a man through her eyelashes. Someone who let her voice go a little flirtatious. Someone who didn't yank her arm out of his grasp but instead, let him continue to make her shiver. Someone invulnerable, who had never lost a thing. "The impression I get is that it tends to be the female, but I'm warning you. Not here. And definitely not me."

Cody kept his thumb moving, a drugging sweep one way, then the other. His dark green gaze was hot and somehow narrow, or maybe it was that she felt as if nothing else existed in the whole wide world. As if the way he looked at her in the middle of a crowded cocktail party was the only thing that could even dream of competing with the vastness of the Montana sky.

"I'm glad to hear it," he said after a while. Maybe it was more than a while. Maybe it was years, and Skylar couldn't say she cared as long as he held on to her like that. "But who said it was a one-night stand?"

"Please." She sounded like that someone else, then. That girl who feared nothing—and certainly not a man like him. "You don't even know my name."

"Skylar. And I knew it that night."

She didn't think he could have—but then she remembered Angelique calling for her, out there in the dark grass.

But the woman who'd taken over her body rolled her eyes. "Well, I didn't know yours."

"You know it now." He didn't quite grin at her, and still, her chest felt tight as if he had. "You can read all my vital statistics on the American Extreme Bull Riders website, if you like. Height. Weight. Wins. If that matters to you."

"I'm not really a buckle bunny," she replied. She nodded at his. "Though it's awfully shiny."

Cody's grip on her shifted, and when he tugged her closer to him, she didn't object. It didn't occur to her to object.

"There's a way to prove that," he said. "Buckle bunnies are almost always one-night stands. Because once they get what they want from one cowboy, off they go to ride another."

"I guess that makes me a buckle bunny, then." This time when she smiled at him, there was nothing fake about it. Skylar opted not to interrogate herself about that. "And to be clear, I'm perfectly fine with the one-night stand thing. I didn't expect I'd ever lay eyes on you again."

The *I didn't* want *to lay eyes on you again* part was implied.

"I get that." That was definitely a smile, then. That curve in the corner of his mouth that only seemed to deepen the longer he looked at her. "But you did."

Skylar was finding it hard to breathe. She felt as if she was wrapped in something shimmery and too hot. And he was still holding on to her. She thought she should say something, but words seemed beyond her. She just watched him, all that granite and steel. And she felt the way his touch reverberated all throughout her body. She told herself she didn't care what happened next.

Because it hadn't occurred to her that there would be a *next.* Skylar hadn't thought in terms of *next* for so long now, that all she wanted to do was revel in the fact that there was a next and it was happening. Right now.

"For one thing, darlin', it wasn't really a one-night stand," Cody said, and his gaze grew somehow even more intent as he maneuvered her an inch or so closer to him, so she could feel all that heat she remembered coming off him in waves. It became a struggle not to touch him the way she wanted. Everywhere. "It wasn't really a night, was it? I think if aspersions are going to be cast and names called, it needs to be longer than an hour on a picnic table. Don't you?"

Chapter Five

CODY HAD NO idea what the hell he was doing.

He'd kept hold of Skylar's wrist and he'd escorted her out of the restaurant, then helped her into his truck like they were on a sweet little date. When he didn't date and wasn't sweet, because why pretend he was interested in anything other than one thing—which he could find a whole lot quicker in a bar? No sweetness required. And now he was driving out of Billings proper as the last of the July light seemed to singe the edges of the Rimrocks with this woman beside him and he had no idea why he hadn't simply nodded politely and then walked away when her father had introduced them.

But that wasn't any kind of explanation.

There was a too-pretty woman sitting in the cab of his truck, with that unreadable, crooked smile aimed out the window as he followed the Yellowstone River out of town. Cody had already had her and he didn't do second helpings. It wasn't worth the hassle. He should have been delighted to hear that she didn't want anything else from him. He should have taken her at her word.

But instead, he'd taken her with him.

Now she was close enough that he could smell her and it was driving him a little crazy. Maybe that was the explanation. It wasn't the spun-sugar scent of her skin that he remembered despite himself, and could still taste, but something else. Maybe a perfume. Maybe whatever soap she used. Either way it was a hint of cedar and something warm, the way sunlight would smell if it could.

And now he was a goddamned poet. What the hell was the matter with him?

Cody needed to turn his truck around and get her away from him before he did something even stupider than this. But he didn't. He didn't even slow down.

"I thought the tour stayed in a hotel," Skylar said. She didn't sound accusing or even particularly worried. She was still staring out the window as if she'd never seen this part of Billings before, and she sounded completely relaxed about the fact that he was driving her away from the city. And all the people. And any kind of safety.

There was no reason that should irritate him. But it did. His voice was clipped and a little too pissed when he answered her.

"The tour does. I don't."

He felt her gaze on him for a moment, but then it was gone again and he hated the fact that he could *feel* anything. Much less that. Her. When he glanced over, she had her fingers laced together in the depression her dress made between her thighs, and he had no idea why that seemed to fall through him like water cascading over rock. As if he'd remember it forever, Skylar Grey in his truck with the last little bit of summer light making her glow, with her hands in her lap and that lopsided smile on her face.

It was like he was in a trance.

Cody shook it off, and tried to figure out what it was about her smile that bugged him so much. Maybe it was because it wasn't quite a smile. Not really. It was just that maddening tilt of her lips in the corners that made her look entirely too satisfied. Too pleased with herself.

As if she knew something he didn't.

"Maybe you should be a little more concerned that I abducted you from the middle of the city and am driving you out to parts unknown," he heard himself say, like a psycho.

She didn't quite laugh, but the sound she made was close enough that he found himself suddenly obsessed with hearing that rusty, surprised, real laughter he'd heard the other night, out there in the woods. He could almost feel the scrape of it again, moving over him like her hands on his skin.

"I wouldn't suggest you do me any harm." This time when she looked his way, she kept that blue gaze of hers on him long enough for him to catch it. "Everybody in that restaurant saw me leave with Cody Galen, veteran star of the American Extreme Bull Riders Tour. I'm sure they're gossiping about it right now. If I don't turn up safe and sound after such a public abduction, you'll spend the weekend explaining yourself to the authorities. I imagine I'm safer with you tonight than I would be with my own father."

He should have found her irritating. He clearly *wanted* to find her irritating.

But instead, Cody was the one to laugh. "Not quite that safe, darlin'."

He could feel the temperature change in the truck. He knew the look he threw at her as he took the road that led out of town was charged. Electric. Filled with all that dark need that had been clawing at him since he'd realized who Billy Grey was taking him across the restaurant to meet.

It had seemed inevitable that it would be her, standing there with her back to the party. And he knew he could have headed the entire interaction off at the pass if he'd wanted. He could have avoided the potential awkwardness and continued doing what passed for his glad-handing routine all around. There'd been no reason to let Billy introduce him to his daughter.

This felt inevitable too. A back road leading out into the middle of nowhere. A pretty girl and all that hunger heating up the space between them. Cody couldn't seem to help himself.

"Why don't you want to stay with the rest of the tour?" she asked after a while. After the lights of Billings had dimmed a bit, and they were driving out on a country road deep into the thick embrace of a Montana summer night.

That wasn't the kind of question he usually answered.

Cody didn't want to think about what it was about her that was so different. He didn't want to *think.* If he hadn't wanted more from her than what he'd already gotten on that picnic table, he would have handled this situation back there in that restaurant. In a bathroom or closet with a lock. Out in an alley, if necessary. He wasn't picky. And he was pretty confident that even if she was, generally speaking, he probably could have convinced her otherwise.

He'd always been a greedy bastard. He'd wanted more than that. And apparently *more than that* came with the kinds of questions he usually refused to entertain.

Of course, Skylar wasn't the tour promoter, forever on his case about the interviews Cody should be doing and the narrative he should be selling to cater to the fans—who apparently found cowboys risking their lives on the backs of animals that could kill them in an instant insufficiently dramatic. She wasn't one of the cloying, drunk women he gravitated toward because it was easy, who giggled instead of asking questions, and knew better than to ask him for more than he gave.

From the sleek way she styled her hair to the dresses she wore, neat and tailored to her body without in any way overtly emphasizing her form, Skylar had *good, decent woman* written all over her. With a touch of something sophisticated besides. And having met her father, Cody figured that came directly from her.

It was the way she held herself, even sitting there in the cab of his truck. She kept her back straight, her hands folded in her lap. She didn't slouch or hunker down in the seat. She didn't prop her feet up on the dashboard. She wasn't a cowgirl, she wasn't a skank, she wasn't even a fan of bull riding as far as he could tell. And yet he couldn't remember ever wanting another woman more.

"Is that a tricky question?" she asked, reminding him that he'd let her question sit there. She didn't actually shrug, but it was there in her voice. "You don't have to tell me if it is."

And he shouldn't have felt disarmed. Out of his depth, when there was almost nothing he was better at than taking a woman home with him. There was no reason that tonight should feel different from a hundred other nights out on tour, from Oklahoma to Washington to Florida and back again, all one big blur. There was no reason Skylar should be any different. There was no reason she should stand out, in perfect focus.

But she was. She did. There was no getting past it.

He'd watched her walk away from him in her father's backyard and he'd thought about little else since. Not something he wanted to admit, but then again, maybe that was why he heard himself talking about things he didn't talk about. Ever.

"The tour is different when you're young," he said gruffly. "You're on the road all the time. You don't have much money, because you're not that good. You have your moments to shine, sure. It's how you got on the tour in the first place and you have to keep your ranking. But sustaining a high score across a weekend, and then a season—that's the hard part."

He barely remembered that kid. All he remembered was the anger. It was all he'd had going for him back then. Anger and his ability to channel it all into eight perfect seconds, just him and a bull in a wild, raw dance.

"Anyone can have one good ride," he said now. "It's having a good ride every time you get on the bull, or most of the time, that makes a career."

"Sounds like the only people who could really understand that would be the people who were doing it right along with you," she ventured. "But maybe I'm missing something."

"My first few years, the other riders were my brothers. Family." He refused to talk about his own family. He couldn't be that far gone, surely. This was bad enough. "But that was a long time ago."

He expected her to comment on that, but she didn't. Because apparently, Skylar didn't do a damn thing that he expected her to do. Cody kept his eyes on the road and his hands on the wheel, and didn't let himself think too much about the fact that his mouth kept moving.

"The best friend I made on the tour is in a wheelchair now. He got carried out of an arena in Texas and he'll never walk again. The others dropped off here and there. A lot of injuries. Surgery after surgery, always thinking the next one might fix what getting stomped on by a pissed-off bull broke. It never does. Or there are babies and wives and a whole lot more concerns about all those concussions, suddenly." He shrugged. "What no one wants to talk about is that sooner or later, you lose the fire for it. And you can't do it without the fire, because all you are then is a crazy man with too many stress fractures who might die if he goes back out there one more time."

He'd never said that out loud before. Cody wasn't sure he could have articulated it quite like that—not to anyone else. Not anywhere else. And now it was out there and all he wanted was to shove it back inside.

But she didn't give him a pep talk. She didn't make sympathetic sounds that he would have found unbearable. She didn't try to commiserate with him.

"Lose the fire of anything," she said after a moment, very matter-of-factly, as if they were talking about the kind of thing everybody did, "and of course it feels like a chore."

Cody rubbed his hand over his chest before he realized what he was doing. He slapped it back on the steering wheel and scowled out into the darkness. "Except the chore in this case is a thousand-pound and then some pissed-off bull who wants to stomp your ass. And will, first chance he gets."

She laughed at that, that scrape of sound that made him think she didn't laugh much, and there was no reason it should make him scowl less.

"I grant you that losing the fire that makes you want to be a barista, for example, just leads to you making a substandard latte," Skylar said. "It's not the same as jumping on a bull. But then again, what is?"

That was the question that had kept him doing it all these years. The question that made him set his jaw and ignore all the minor, survivable agonies that would take other men down. What got him to tape himself up and do it night after night. He liked the money. He liked to win. He liked that he'd been able to help his half-sisters. But he'd always loved the sport.

"It's easy to fall out of love with bull riding, Skylar," he said now. "Because everything hurts, always, and torn ligaments and broken bones are just all in a weekend's ride. Win or lose, you're still gonna hurt."

She shifted beside him, but she didn't say anything, and he kept going. Like this was some kind of confessional, the dark road outside his truck and the quiet within. That scent of hers: cedar and sun. That thing in his chest that was clawing its way out whether he wanted it to or not.

"You're always on the road. City after city until you can't tell the difference between them and don't even care. One hotel room after another until you forget where you are or that you ever had roots somewhere else. And the truth is that you can do everything right. You can train and test yourself, eat right and practice, get your head right and still get a bull who isn't in the mood to do his part. That leaves you busted up and pissed off and hundreds of miles from home for nothing. That's the life." He sighed. "I'm sick of the life."

"I hope that's not a cry for help." But her voice was light. Soft and teasing. And with that other thread in it that pricked at him, as if he should understand it. Recognize it, when he didn't. Or didn't want to. "I don't want to see you doing a little suicide by Bushwacker tomorrow night."

He was talking about things he didn't talk about. This whole night had been him behaving in a way he didn't behave. And still, his lips twitched at that. "Bushwacker retired years ago."

And had never been one of the legendary bulls on the American Extreme Bull Riders Tour, but he didn't point that out.

"I'm sure he has a successor who's just as mean." Skylar let out that rusty little laugh, and he didn't get how it was more effective than another woman's hands all over him. He didn't understand what she was doing to him. "There's never any shortage of ornery bulls."

"Maybe not." He shook his head, because this strange trance that still had him in its grip had to go. "But I do take some pride in being the most ornery bull rider on the tour."

Another laugh. "Is there a lot of competition for the title?"

"No, ma'am, there is not. Because I dominate in all things, but that especially." Cody could have kept it light.

Funny. He didn't know why he didn't. "I keep to myself. I don't need more friends I'm going to have to visit in hospitals, then have to lie to when I tell them they'll be fine. No more graves I'm going to have to stand over. No more. This is my last season."

He hadn't said that out loud either to anyone but his mother, and not so starkly. He was in his thirties, which made him ancient in bull-riding circles. He got asked all the time what his retirement plans were and how much longer he thought he'd stay and fight, and he always mouthed something noncommittal. Except here. With her.

Of course.

Skylar didn't say anything, and he couldn't tell if it was because she didn't understand the magnitude of what he'd told her or possibly didn't care. He didn't think it was that second one, but what did he know? Still, a kind of agitation gnawed at him as he turned off the main road and followed the dirt track that wound its way down to a deserted little field near the river. His headlights picked up his Airstream right where he'd left it, looking sleek and shiny in the dark.

"Oh," she said softly. "You bring your roots with you on tour. That makes sense."

Cody would never have put it that way.

"I like to be alone," he muttered. He pulled up to the trailer and turned the truck off and for a moment they sat there in the dark.

"Change is hard," Skylar said while his eyes were still adjusting. "No matter what. No matter why. It's always, always hard. Believe me, I understand."

"I didn't intend to get philosophical," he told her then. "Or whatever this was. I think I was pretty clear that my intention was to get laid. Repeatedly. All night long, in fact, despite the fact I need my sleep."

This time, she really laughed, and there was nothing rusty about it. It filled up the cab of the truck, and his chest, too.

"Well, thank goodness this long drive out into the middle of nowhere didn't get awkward or anything," she said, her voice thick with that laughter. It felt like her hands all over him. "I mean think what could have happened. All those dark promises of a night of passion—a full one this time, to separate it from the other night, which for some reason couldn't stand on its own. And instead it's all become metaphor and philosophy and how bull riding is life, really. Except more painful. And here we are, down by a river near a lonely old trailer like a country song." She shook her head, and more of that scent filled the air between them, making him feel hollowed out with need. "And I know you must know that a country song never ends well, especially for a cowboy."

Cody laughed at that. Her. He didn't question it. And he didn't think about what he was doing. He just reached over and got his hands on her, at last. *At last.* He hauled her toward him, down the bench seat and then up onto his lap, and then finally—*finally*—he shut himself up, and put his mouth where it belonged. On hers.

She tasted better than he remembered, and in his memory she was spectacular.

It was all fire. Sugar and flame. She was sweet and she was hot and she didn't play any games. She wrapped her arms around his neck as she fought to get closer to him. She angled her jaw and took him deeper, as if she was mimicking what she knew was going to happen later. What needed to happen now.

Him deep inside her, forever, if he could swing it.

But here, now, he reveled in the feel of her on his lap. This pretty thing, this unreadable woman, who made a lot more sense to him when she was making those greedy little noises in the back of her throat.

It almost hurt to pull his mouth from hers. But he did it.

"Let me guess," she whispered against his mouth, and moved a little on his lap in emphasis. "You're going to tell me some more about that one good ride."

She was going to kill him. And he was going to like it.

But it wasn't going to happen in his damn truck.

Cody wrenched open his door and climbed out, pulling her with him. It wasn't the slickest move he'd ever made, but he didn't much care when she just let herself fall against him, the soft weight of her as welcome as a touch. Better.

He even found himself holding her hand, taking it in his as he walked toward the trailer. But she only went a few steps, then stopped. She pulled back against his hand and he realized she was tipping her head back to stare up at the night sky.

"You can't ignore the stars," she told him when he stopped walking too. "There are people in places all over the world who look up and don't see anything. The lights of the city they live in, maybe. Their neighbor's house. But not *this*."

Cody couldn't remember the last time he'd looked at the damn stars. Deliberately, anyway. But that was the trouble with Skylar. She kept getting under his skin. He couldn't seem to resist her and that was no good. He knew it. She was the kind of trouble he knew he didn't want.

But he didn't do anything about it. He didn't toss her back in his truck and drive her back into town, then wash his hands of her the way he knew he should. Instead, he moved so he could wrap his arms around her, like somebody's boyfriend, and he tipped his own head back to stare at the stars along with her.

Like he was that guy.

And then he made it worse, because they stood there like that for a long time.

"I lived in Atlanta for years," she said, softly.

Maybe she was yelling, he couldn't tell. Bright and wild, the sky was so dirty with stars it was as if someone had spilled them everywhere and forgotten to come pick them up again. The summer night was cluttered with them. So bright it seemed like they were pressing down from above. Hell, maybe she screamed. Cody wasn't sure he could tell the difference when the night sky was making such a ruckus.

"I never had any intention of coming home to Montana, not to live," Skylar continued. "If you'd asked me I would have told you a million reasons why I preferred to live in the city. Why it was the better choice for me. It was such a big city, bustling with people and things and restaurants and stores. Everything your heart could desire and more, and I loved it. But it didn't have this." She let out a sigh that seemed to come from deep inside of her, and Cody found himself holding her tighter. "I know the sky is everywhere but in Montana, it's different. It's closer. Bigger."

Later, Cody would never know if she was the one who turned around or if he was the one who turned her around to face him, because he couldn't take any more. But it didn't matter. Because somehow or other she was turned around and they were facing each other, and then his mouth was on hers again.

Every time he kissed her it felt as if it had been years. Long, crappy years since the last time, and he was finally making it right.

And as bright as the stars were above them, Skylar burned brighter. She was hot and much too wild, and he couldn't keep his hands to himself. He didn't really try. He traced his way down the line of her back, then got his hands on her sweet butt. She nipped his lip and he pulled her closer, reveling in the crush of her breasts against the wall of his chest.

Then he was taking her down with him, down into the field where they'd been standing, because he needed to get horizontal with her. Immediately.

He rolled her over so she was sitting astride him, laughing a little bit, and he thought it was the best sound he'd ever heard. She reached down and pulled up her dress, tugging it up and over her head and then throwing it aside. She did the same with her bra and then there she was. Covered in starlight and even more beautiful than he remembered. More beautiful than anyone should be. Cody got his hands in her hair, he got his mouth between her breasts, and then he took his time learning her the way he wanted.

God, the way she tasted. One nipple as velvety as the next, and the noises she made when he sucked each one into his mouth about killed him. He was so hard it hurt.

She tilted her head back as he sucked on her, rocking her hips as if she couldn't help herself as she rode him a little. But when he released her, she returned her attention to him. She ran her hands down his chest and let out a small sigh that sounded like happiness. She took her time unbuttoning his shirt, pulling open the sides to expose his skin and then bending forward to perform her own little acts of torture down the length of his torso. She pulled the ends of his shirt out of his waistband and then moved toward his buckle, and he didn't do a single thing to stop her.

And any lingering doubts he might have had about her interest in the buckle itself disappeared, because she couldn't seem to open it fast enough. No stopping to admire the win it heralded or to request a selfie, as one recent conquest had. Her hands were actually trembling as she pulled down his zipper and pulled him out, and he didn't think it was trepidation. He thought it was the same insane hunger that stormed through him.

As if they were both just as pummeled by this thing.

She looked up at him, that crooked smile of hers enough to make his cock ache, and then she made it worse. Her hands gripped him as she shifted herself down, knelt between his thighs, and then bent to suck in the head. Just the head, as if she needed a taste to go on.

Then she looked up at him again.

"I want to taste you," she whispered, in case he'd missed her clear intention.

And Cody was only a man. Not a very good one. And certainly not selfless enough to turn down her mouth. Who was he to deny a lady?

"Don't let me stop you, darlin'," he said lazily, and stretched out in the grass as she smiled at him, then sucked him in deep.

He let himself go as she played with him. She tested his length, sucking him in and then licking him when she pulled her head back. She moved her hips back and forth as she worked him, as if the same fire was building in her. And

Cody lost himself in the wet heat of her. He sank his fingers into that silky dark hair of hers and met her rhythm. She sucked harder, took him deeper.

And he groaned out her name when he came.

When she crawled her way up to sit over him again, she was smiling.

He wasn't sure his heart could take this. Cody had never wasted much time worrying about whether a perfect woman existed, but Skylar was proving him wrong, one crooked smile after the next. And he didn't want to think through the implications of that. At this moment, out here in the dark with only the stars as witness, he didn't care.

"My turn," he growled.

He took his time laying her out on the grass beneath him. He pulled another pair of sexy little boy shorts off her hips, tugging them down along the length of her smooth legs and then casting them aside. And as he knelt back to get rid of his shirt and the rest of his clothes, he just looked at her. Lying there with the stars all over her, her arms tossed up over her head. She had her head thrown back as if there was a wind on her face, when the night was still. And that crooked, satisfied smile that made him feel things he didn't know how to name.

Cody wanted more. He wanted everything.

He settled for getting himself between those sweet thighs of hers. He kissed his way down her body, reacquainting himself with those buttery nipples and the way her belly trembled just slightly when he played with her navel. He shouldered his way between her thighs, pulling her knees up so her legs hung down his back, and she was already gasping for air.

"I haven't done anything yet," he teased her, his voice a low rumble.

"I feel pretty sure that you will."

He proved her right. He set his mouth to that perfect pussy of hers, already so wet and slick and sweet that the taste about made him crazy.

But he was a man who rode giant, largely untamed animals for fun and profit, so he could certainly handle a little crazy.

Cody took his time. He licked his way into her and learned every last contour of that sweet little pussy. He let her move her hips beneath him, crying out her need into the night. He played with her clit until she sobbed. He found every last little sweet spot that made her buck up against him and hiss a little and hold her breath. And when she really got going, call out his name.

She tugged on his head, her fingers clenched deep in his hair, and he loved the little sting of it. He also loved ignoring her. He licked where he wanted. Sometimes he used his fingers.

And every time she came, bucking and crying and rolling all over him, drumming his back with her heels, she did it in his mouth.

And when she was limp and gasping, so breathless she couldn't form any more words—or at least not any he could understand, he crawled back up the length of that sweet body of hers, covered her with his, rolled on a condom and finally thrust himself deep inside of her.

He'd wanted fast, dirty. He'd thought that was the promise they'd made, insofar as they'd promised each other anything, back in that restaurant. But this wasn't that.

This wasn't anything like that.

Cody didn't know what to call this.

It was slow. Intense. She wrapped her legs around his hips and her arms around his neck, and she met him. She met his every thrust, she took him so deep it made his head spin, and together they became one bright, gleaming thing, like the sky so quiet and full above them.

Too bright. Too full.

Until Cody couldn't tell which was which.

And this time, when she hurtled over that edge and started to shake apart, he went with her.

Chapter Six

SKYLAR DIDN'T KNOW who was more surprised when she walked into the house early the next morning, her or Angelique, who was standing there in the great front foyer with a pile of laundry in her arms when the door opened.

Not laundry, Skylar corrected herself as she eased the door closed behind her with a soft click. It looked like one of the throws that was usually over the back of one of the couches in the family room, and it didn't take a private eye like Veronica Mars to figure out that Lacey or Layla had probably spilled something on it. Or vomited on it. Or any of the many other things little kids could do in seconds to render everything sticky and in need of a good wash.

Angelique stared. Skylar stared back, and tried out a little smile to ease the awkwardness.

While outside there was no pretending that wasn't a big truck pulling away from the curb in front of the house, then roaring off into the dark this side of dawn.

"It's bad enough that you're so pretty in the middle of the day when you've had time to do things," Skylar said in as casual a voice as she could muster while she was wearing last night's dress and letting her sandals hang from one finger. She didn't want to think about the state of her hair. And anyway, it happened to be true. Angelique was ridiculously beautiful around the clock. Tall, leggy, with long brown hair piled into a messy bun on top of her head. She wore yoga pants and a tank top at five-thirty in the morning, just rolled out of bed and clearly already elbow deep in handling her twin girls, and looked better than Skylar did after hours of preparation. "But why do you look so good when it's barely dawn?"

Angelique blinked. "I thought you were upstairs. In bed."

Skylar pushed away from the front door and walked further into the house, still smiling. Because she thought that if she let the smile slip, everything else would fall apart too, maybe.

"No," she said. And that was all.

She'd never done the infamous walk of shame before. She hadn't slept with Thayer until they'd been together for a while and he'd had his own apartment that she'd practically lived in. There had been no walking back somewhere with the night before all over her. She almost wished there had been—it would have meant she hadn't wasted all that time waiting. Waiting and waiting to honor a future they'd never have.

She expected the very thought of Thayer to wash through her like an indictment, but it didn't. All she could think about was Cody. What they'd done out in that field. And then inside that streamlined, gorgeous Airstream that had felt like him. Exactly like him. All those clean, masculine lines and yet surprisingly comfortable despite that.

Skylar was a little surprised she could even stand. She hadn't gotten much in the way of sleep. And a whole lot more exercise than her usual three-mile run that was more often a walk.

"Skylar." Angelique's voice sounded something a whole lot like scandalized. Appalled, even, which made Skylar's skin feel tight. "You weren't with… Not that bull rider?"

What Skylar wanted to do was crawl into bed and sleep for a few hours, but she knew that wasn't going to happen. Even if she somehow fast-forwarded through this unexpected inquisition, her father liked to get up pretty early himself and would no doubt want a head start getting ready for the weekend at the arena. She could *maybe* catch a little catnap—that was all. If she went and crawled into bed right now.

But Angelique followed her when she walked toward the kitchen in the back of the house, and she decided she needed coffee to deal with this. Whatever this was. She tossed her sandals by the back door and then padded over to the coffeemaker, which in a house with small children was always programmed for five a.m. She heard Angelique go into the laundry room and then come out again, and she wasn't surprised to find her stepmother on the other side of the kitchen island after she dumped enough hazelnut creamer into her giant mug of coffee to sugar up the world.

Not happy, certainly. But not surprised.

Especially because Angelique didn't look appalled. Or horrified. She looked *concerned.*

"This isn't you," she said quietly.

Skylar took a long pull from her coffee and let it work its magic. Because it was that or throw it at her stepmother.

"I don't know what that means."

"You don't run off and spend the night with random bull riders." Angelique wasn't the sort to wear pearls, but if she had been, she'd be clutching them then. And something in Skylar knotted up into a hard ball. "If your father comes down here and sees you in last night's dress I think he'll have a heart attack."

Skylar counted to ten. She reminded herself that she wasn't a misbehaving fifteen-year-old and even if she had been, this woman wasn't her mother. Then she did it again because the first round didn't take.

"I appreciate your concern, Angelique, I do." She sounded much more Southern when she was pissed, and she was pretty sure she sounded like a magnolia tree or a mint julep right about then.

"Did he take advantage of you?"

"What?" Skylar snapped her mug down on the counter and stared. "Do I look taken advantage of?"

"You're not the sort of person who runs off with a man

like that, that's all."

"A man like what?" Skylar asked, maybe a little dangerously. "And I'm not sure what kind of person you think I am in this scenario. A very spineless one, apparently?"

But Angelique didn't seem to hear her. "I never dated any cowboys, but I can't imagine they're much different from any other athletes and believe me, I know how they are sometimes."

"We're not dating, Angelique." Skylar smiled then, but it wasn't a nice smile. It hurt her cheeks, but it was better than the bitter thing she was biting back. "What we're doing or not doing isn't anyone's business but ours."

Angelique sighed, and the unfairness of this whole thing gnawed at Skylar. Aside from the fact that this was no one's business but hers, Skylar was the only member of the entire, extended Grey family who hadn't openly condemned Angelique and Billy when they'd gotten together. She'd bitten her tongue and kept her thoughts to herself, because everyone involved was an adult and none of those adults were her or someone who'd made promises to her.

How quickly people forgot.

"Skylar, come on." Angelique folded her arms across her middle and clearly *tried* to look patient. It was the *trying* that made Skylar's temper roar in her ears. "You've been through a really dark time. It's not actually surprising that you might give in to a few self-destructive impulses—"

"I had sex with a remarkably good-looking man. I didn't

go on a meth bender and wake up in a prison cell with blood on my hands," Skylar snapped. She regretted the words instantly, but it was too late. She'd not only had her first walk of shame, she'd also become the sort of person who screeched about her sex life in public, like an animal. *Kill me now.* "And this may come as a shock to you and the conservative morals I was unaware you held dear until this morning, but sex isn't particularly self-destructive."

Sex with Cody was life-altering in a completely different way, and certainly destructive—but not in the way Angelique meant it. And there was no need to get into all that now. Especially when Skylar hadn't had any time to process it herself.

"I feel like this is my fault." Angelique sounded genuinely sad and that made it worse. It put Skylar's teeth on edge. "I thought you needed your space, so I gave it to you. I thought that was the right thing to do."

Skylar fought to keep herself under control, which wasn't as easy as it should have been, because she wasn't as numb as she'd been for the last couple of years. Something else to think about when she wasn't busy defending herself.

"I'm not a teenager who had a bad breakup and is now acting out after school." She thought she deserved a medal for that even, cool tone. "And I mean this in the nicest way possible, Angelique, but I didn't ask for your input."

"You have to realize this isn't who you are," Angelique insisted, her brow creased with concern.

Real concern.

"Who am I?" Skylar demanded, and that even, cool tone was gone as if it had never been. "Who do you think I am? Because let me tell you something, I think you're talking to a person who doesn't exist anymore."

"I know this isn't the way you act, that's all. You're careful. You consider things from every angle and you don't jump into anything rashly."

"True story," Skylar agreed hotly, something bubbling up from a dark well inside of her she hadn't known was there. But once she started, she couldn't stop, even though the things that were pelting out from that place unnerved her. "And what did that get me? I waited and waited and waited. I planned everything so carefully. Thayer and I were together for eight years. *Eight years.* We could have been living the life we were planning instead of just talking about it happening *someday.* You'll forgive me if I'm not quite so hot on the virtues of *careful consideration* these days."

"Thayer—"

"Is dead." Skylar knew the starkness of that should have taken her knees out. It should have felt like a punch to the gut. But if it did, she didn't feel it, because whatever was inside of her was stronger. It was a storm and it was sweeping her along with it as it raged and the funny thing was, she didn't have it in her to mind. "*He is dead.* I tried to pretend otherwise and guess what? He's still dead. He's never coming back. No one knows that more than I do, Angelique."

"He was so nice," her stepmother said, her voice rough, as if she was emotional too. As if all of this hurt her, somehow.

But Skylar had been soothing the fractured emotions of other people about her own damned loss for two years too long. She was over it.

"He was," she agreed, and she wasn't sure if she didn't sound like herself at all or if she sounded more like herself at that moment than she had in years. "He was very nice. He was funny and he was kind and he lit up the room when he walked into it. People wanted to be around him and I felt lucky that he wanted to be with me. There are stories about me only he could tell and he never will again and do you know what that feels like? I'll tell you. It feels like all the parts of me that only he knew died with him. But I didn't." She slapped her palm against the counter in front of her, as much to see if she could feel the sting as for emphasis. "*I* didn't."

"What the hell is going on?" Skylar didn't turn toward her father's half-sleepy, half-annoyed voice as he walked into the room. She kept her gaze on her stepmother. "Jesus Christ, Skylar, did you just get in?"

Angelique didn't actually say *I told you so.* Her expression did it for her.

But Skylar had already had enough. And her palm hurt.

"I'm not going to defend myself to either one of you," she said, and she left her coffee behind as she started for the stairs. She thought she should have been shaking, but she wasn't. On the contrary, she wasn't sure she'd ever felt quite so calm.

One more thing to process when she got a minute to breathe.

"You can't stay out all night—" her father began as Skylar walked past him, skirting him by a wide, possibly dramatic margin as she made for the stairs.

"Why can't I?" She turned toward him as she said it, and didn't back down. "Give me one good reason."

"This is my house," Billy threw at her, which was like a trip down memory lane. She remembered him yelling exactly that at Jesse years ago. That teenage, Goody-Two-Shoes version of her would never have believed she'd ever give him cause to say it to her.

"Then I'll move out sooner than planned. Problem solved. I'll start packing as soon as I get upstairs."

Billy rolled his eyes. "Maybe take the drama down a notch or two."

"I'm being practical, not theatrical. You have every right to dictate how people behave under your roof." She shrugged. "I have every right to find another roof."

"Skylar, I'm not trying to make you feel bad," Angelique said from over by the kitchen island. "But I would hope that if the situations were reversed you'd give me a heads-up if you saw me running straight for a cliff."

"A cliff," Skylar repeated. She looked from her father to

her stepmother. Then again, but neither one of them backed down. "You mean, like the time you came home for Christmas—"

"That was different," Angelique said tightly.

"Leave it alone, Skylar," her father growled, because of course, the cliff in question was him.

"You're right," Skylar agreed, locking eyes with Angelique and ignoring her father. "It's a lot different. You were actually cheating on my brother when you hooked up with my father under the same roof. This roof, in point of fact. The difference is, I'm not cheating on anyone."

She wanted to add, *because* I *wouldn't do something like that* but didn't, and thought she deserved applause for her restraint. She headed for the stairs instead, aware that there was some kind of marital communication going on behind her, but she didn't care what it was. There was nowhere good this conversation could go. She wanted it over.

"You got me," Angelique said from behind her, and it made Skylar's stomach ache to hear the hurt tone of her voice. "Your father and I are terrible people. But we're not talking about us and the stupid things we did that caused pain all around. We're not talking about things neither one of us can change. We're talking about you."

"*You* are talking about me." Skylar stopped at the foot of the stairs and looked back over her shoulder. "*I* didn't want to have this conversation."

"Thayer wouldn't have wanted to see you turn into just

another buckle bunny," her father blurted out then. As if he'd even known Thayer beyond family gatherings over the years. As if he was the last remaining defender of Thayer's interests on this earth—or hell, any kind of decent father himself. "Neither do I."

Something inside of her snapped. Skylar turned, very slowly, and glared at the two of them. So hard she was surprised her head didn't tear open.

"I'm going to ignore the amazing hypocrisy flying around here this morning," she said, very distinctly. "The fact that you opened up your home and let me stay here is wonderful, but it doesn't give you the right to comment on my life or how I live it. I could have spent years commenting on your all's, but I didn't."

"I'm your father," Billy protested.

"And I'm not the daughter you think you know," Skylar retorted. She waved a hand over her surprisingly uncrumpled dress, trying to encompass all of her. "I'm not the same person I was two years ago and I never will be. That's not sad. That's just a fact. If Thayer was alive we wouldn't be having this conversation. I wouldn't be here. But he's not. And I have to figure out who I am and what I want without him. That might not be pretty and guess what? You don't have to watch."

"Skylar." Angelique shook her head. "You can't tell me some bull rider with a death wish—and don't kid yourself, they all have a death wish, they *ride bulls*—is a logical first step in your new life."

"My life, Angelique," Skylar replied tightly. And maybe a little loudly, so there could be no doubt. "*Mine.* And if I want to sleep with the entire American Extreme Bull Riders Tour, I will. Whether you're worried about me or not."

Chapter Seven

"I DON'T ACTUALLY want to sleep with the entire tour," Skylar told her father tersely, many hours later, and resented the fact that she had to say it at all. But she'd had time to think about throwing that ridiculous thing at him and storming off, very much like the teenager she wasn't, and regretted it. It made her look like a spiteful child. "In case you were actually concerned that was a possibility."

"For the love of all that is holy, I don't want to talk about who my daughter is sleeping with," Billy retorted immediately, sounding as if he was being tortured. Or would prefer a round or two of torture to this. "I don't even want to think about it. I'd rather pound nails into my own head."

They were both standing in the Grey Sport booth in the Rimrocks Auto Arena, where they'd been pointedly not making eye contact ever since the doors had opened and the people had started pouring in ahead of that night's show. Before that, they'd managed to not discuss anything directly all day. They'd sold their specially branded tour apparel and the usual collection of rural-edged sportswear that the local farmers and ranchers and the ever-growing community of

Billings hipsters might wear, ironically or otherwise.

But now the show was due to start any second, which meant they were supposed to leave the booth in the hands of Billy's genial manager—who'd been working overtime to pretend she didn't notice the chilly weather between Billy and Skylar today—and take their seats in the much-coveted VIP section Grey Sports had gotten as a perk of sponsorship.

Skylar thought she might have to go ahead and throw herself at the mercy of one of the bulls if she had to sit in the stands in this same barbed, unpleasant silence, surrounded by other local folks with VIP tickets who knew the both of them and would be paying attention to what went on between them.

Or maybe only knew Skylar as the woman who'd gone off with that bull rider last night.

It had been bad enough to spend the whole day pretending not to notice the speculative glances thrown her way everywhere she'd gone, particularly here in the arena. The conversations that ground to a halt when she approached. The whispers when her back was turned.

Because, of course, that cocktail party had been for *local* vendors, and they all knew her. Or Billy. Or both of them, plus the rest of the family besides, because the Greys had been a part of Montana forever.

There was probably a consensus going around that Skylar did, in fact, plan to sleep her way through the whole of the tour and might have made a big dent in that goal last night.

Leaving from that party with Cody was as good as taking out a full-page ad in the *Billings Gazette.* The only upside was the fact that today was the first day since she'd returned to Montana that no one had told her how sorry they were for her loss.

Baby steps, Skylar thought resolutely.

"I never wanted to talk about it with you either, Dad," Skylar pointed out now, and it was a struggle to make her voice sound that reasonable.

"Angelique was just trying to look out for you," her father retorted, his jaw set in a mulish line.

She reminded herself that this wasn't about being *right,* it was about being *comfortable,* and that wasn't going to happen tonight if Billy was nursing this grudge the whole time.

You could leave, a sharp little voice inside reminded her. And yes, she could.

But Cody was riding tonight and did it make Skylar everything Angelique had accused her of being if she wanted to watch him?

"I really appreciate that," she said. Still aiming for *calm* and *reasonable.* "I do. But I'm fine."

Still, the look Billy was giving her didn't change. "And since when do you throw all that old junk in my face, Skylar? I thought we were past that."

She was saved from answering that by the sound of the usual American Extreme Bull Riders spectacle beginning out there in the arena. The crowd went wild and the music blared.

Billy glared at her another minute, then jerked his chin in a mute demand to follow him. Skylar wanted to march off in the other direction, but that would be cutting off her nose to spite her face, and she'd never seen the point of gestures like that. Especially not when she had a vested interest in keeping nose and face attached.

Instead, she followed her father from their booth. He led her along the arena's long corridor and then down into to the VIP section that was almost all the way on the dirt floor, with a direct line of sight to all the chutes. So close that they wouldn't have to look up at the big screens to see what was going on—it was going to happen right there. Right in front of them.

Thousand-pound-plus bulls, fired up and ready to party, with all those tough, steely riders clamped on top of them, bursting out into their eight seconds of a struggle—a beautiful, brutal dance, if they were lucky—barely more than six feet away.

Even before she'd known a bull rider personally, Skylar had found that watching the sport made her edgy. Exhilarated and invested about three seconds into every ride. Tonight it felt a whole lot worse.

Or better.

Billy found their seats, three rows up from the dirt, and they settled into them. The crowd went wild for all the riders as they marched out, dressed in their competition shirts and cowboy hats. They all looked fierce and handsome, the baby-faced newbies and longtime stars of the tour alike. The announcers read off Cody's statistics as he walked out to take his turn in the spotlight, and Skylar had to swallow hard as he lifted his black hat to the crowd. He looked grim and focused, the way she supposed he always did, but she had an entirely new appreciation of that expression now.

The man gave *intent* new meaning.

The last time she'd seen him, he'd had the same look on his face when he'd kissed her before she climbed out of his truck. She shivered, because that memory was a gateway for a cascade of other ones, each more vivid than the last. But she controlled it in the next instant, because the last thing she wanted was to attract any more of her father's attention.

There was a prayer for everyone's safety—bulls and riders alike—a callout to the nation's active military and veterans, and then the Star-Spangled Banner was belted out by a local girl who looked all of sixteen, with big curls and a voice to match.

And then it began.

Skylar couldn't even count how many times she'd watched bull riding before. Hundreds of times growing up, right here in Billings. Maybe more than hundreds, if she thought about the rodeos she'd attended out west in Marietta, the little town in Paradise Valley where another huge swathe of Grey family members lived. And had done since the original Grey had hoofed it out of Boston to avoid a crisis or two of his own making, way back in the 1800s. She hadn't been to a rodeo or a bull-riding event like this one in a long time, it was true, but it was the same as she remembered.

More than that—it almost felt like coming home. The rich scent of the dirt, and the more complex note of horses and bulls beneath it were a complicated kind of nostalgia. Country music playing loud in a stadium filled with red, white and blue everything, beer and hot dogs, ads for Ariat, Carhartt, farm equipment, and big old trucks, all made her heart swell a bit. And star-struck little kids and grumpy old men alike, all of them were on their feet and cheering every time the clock ticked toward those golden eight seconds while the rider kept his seat.

Skylar had always liked the sport, but she'd never felt so *personally* about any of it before. Every time a cowboy was thrown, she flinched. Every time a cowboy showed how tough he was by standing up from something that would have laid out the entire Atlanta Falcons defensive line, she couldn't seem to look away from the way he'd limp out of the dirt.

Because she knew what Cody looked like naked, now. Golden and gleaming—and covered in scars. Surgeries, broken bones, cuts and bruises. She'd seen the cabinet in his bathroom, filled with tape and braces and a hundred different ointments for this or that ailment, ache, stiffness, whatever. She'd run her hands over old scars cut with new ones, and had seen the toll that the previous week's show in South Dakota had taken on him, stamped all over his skin.

And tonight she saw exactly how those injuries happened, in case her imagination hadn't been sufficient the night before.

Not that she hadn't known that this was a dangerous sport. Of course she had. Everyone knew it was dangerous. That was part of its appeal. She knew it was why fans loved it. She assumed the riders did too. Not because they had death wishes the way Angelique had claimed, but because it was hard not to love a rush like that.

Or so she assumed, having had the wildest rush of her life with Cody. Repeatedly.

Tonight, standing there watching bull after bull buck and roll and go wild, Skylar felt the danger of it all deep in the pit of her stomach, as if it was happening *to* her. Because it turned out she had a vivid imagination, after all. It was too easy to imagine Cody getting stomped. Cody getting thrown. Cody getting dragged.

She hid another shudder when the medical team raced out to carry one of the riders out. And maybe she cheered a little louder than necessary when the rider climbed to his feet instead, waved to the crowd, and walked off without requiring that gurney after all.

"Date who you want to date," Billy said gruffly during a lull, when the bull fighters were trying to chase a recalcitrant bull back into the chutes, complete with a lasso the bull flat-out ignored.

As if they'd been in the middle of a debate on the subject.

Skylar forced herself to unclench her teeth. She tucked her hands in the back pockets of her jeans to keep herself from clenching them into fists—or swinging them. And she rocked back on the heels of her cowboy boots as if that would give her the sort of calm the bull riders exuded so effortlessly.

"I'm not dating anyone, Dad," she said.

That was the most ridiculous part of all of this. Skylar had stood her ground and thrown herself into the fight because of the principle of it all. Not the reality. The reality was that Cody Galen had never made her a single promise outside of enjoying a whole night together instead of their single encounter on a picnic table.

And Skylar might not have done a lot of dating, but she'd watched the rise and fall and near miss of all her friends' relationships in Atlanta. She'd soothed more than one broken heart on her couch with ice cream in one hand and a friend's cell phone in the other, to cut down on ill-considered, potentially embarrassing calls, texts, and messages. She knew how these things went. The bottom line was that she knew better than to expect anything from a man like Cody. She would be very surprised if she heard from him again. Ever.

But that hadn't been the point this morning. It wasn't the point now.

Just like that raw thing deep inside her wasn't the point either. She'd have to deal with that later. Out there in the brand-new life she knew she had to create, just as soon as she got through this weekend.

Billy ran a hand over his face, and then eyed her for a moment that dragged on too long. As if he'd never seen her before. And maybe that was the real point in all of this, as she'd claimed it was this morning when she'd been a little more volatile than she felt right now. He really hadn't.

She wasn't the same person she'd been and random bull riders had nothing to do with it.

"I'm not going to stand here and pretend to be on any moral high ground," Billy said gruffly after what felt like forever. "That would be ridiculous. I've made more than my share of mistakes."

That was one more award she wouldn't be getting, Skylar thought then, when she managed to keep her face expressionless. She did not throw her mother in his face. She did not bring up Risa, her horrible ex-stepmother, who still lived in Billings and hated Billy with all the fury of a Montana winter. Every winter. She did not mention the many girlfriends she'd known about over the years, not all of them while her father was single.

She kept her mouth shut and waited for sainthood. Or at least an acknowledgment of her restraint.

But Billy only forged on. "But I'm also not going to explain myself to you."

Skylar nodded. "My feelings exactly."

He looked at her, then back toward the dirt of the arena, crossing his arms over his chest. He'd always been a good-looking man. So good-looking, in fact, that Skylar's high school friends had called him *the hot dad,* to her eternal mortification. And her college friends had been more descriptive, on occasion. But those had been his unhappier days. There was no denying that he was calmer lately. More settled.

And, likely because his wife was so much younger than him and objectively stunning, a whole lot fitter. He went for a run every morning and to a CrossFit gym three times a week, which he'd wanted to talk to Skylar about, of course. At length. Obviously, she'd declined the offer. But standing there in the stadium, she was forced to face the uncomfortable fact that her father—*her father*—was cut. Ripped, even.

She was going to have to ruin Scottie's week by texting her about it. As soon as possible.

Well. As soon as Billy stopped having this serious conversation with her.

"No matter what version of yourself you are these days, Skylar, I don't think you meant to hurt Angelique's feelings," he said.

And Skylar stopped composing texts in her head, because that hit her harder than she would have liked. She liked

Angelique—when she ignored the fact that a woman her age was married to her father and was the mother of her half-sisters. She didn't want to hurt her stepmother's feelings. After she'd showered and thought about it a bit this morning, she'd even come to the conclusion that Angelique had meant well. She believed that.

"Of course not," she gritted out.

Because Angelique might indeed have meant well, but that still didn't make it any of her business.

"You know she considers you a friend," her father continued in that same gruff, too-serious voice, possibly pissed off *because* he was being so gruff and serious. "You particularly, because your brother and sister aren't exactly open to that."

Skylar supposed it would be churlish to point out that Jesse was unlikely to ever consider the ex-girlfriend who'd cheated on him with his own father a buddy, even these days when there'd been a noticeable thaw from his direction. In general, anyway. His fiancée Michaela might have taken the edge off, but exactly how friendly was he supposed to be?

Meanwhile, Scottie was a very busy, high-powered lawyer in San Francisco with an even busier and more high-powered lawyer as a live-in boyfriend. When she and Damon weren't locked in their offices for days, they took intensely private vacations in places that required three planes and a watercraft to reach. Scottie had never been off her phone long enough while at family events to develop a relationship with Angelique and that, Skylar had always thought, was a blessing. For Angelique. Because Scottie wasn't a lawyer by accident. She'd honed her cross-examination skills on Risa, the stepmother from hell. She'd cut Angelique down in three sentences, given the opportunity.

Making nice had always been Skylar's role. She was the middle child. The peacemaker. Something that had been easy enough to do with a smile and a busy life far away in Atlanta.

Now that she thought about it, she'd played that role a bit down in Atlanta, too. She'd soothed Thayer when his family got to him and in return she'd smoothed things over with his mother and sisters on the "girls' day" shopping and spa adventures they'd loved so much.

Skylar couldn't really say she missed all that. Maybe, just once, she'd like the chance to be the person everyone tied themselves in knots trying to placate. Maybe she'd like to see what it was like to be a wild card instead of a sure thing.

"She wasn't trying to act like a parent this morning," her father was saying, and the truth about his furious silence all day dawned on her. He really didn't care—or was choosing to ignore—that Skylar had stayed out all night. What he was pissed about was that she'd fought with Angelique. "Believe me, she knows better. She was just worried about you."

That sense of injustice swamped her again, but she took in a deep breath and opted not to let it seize control the way it had this morning.

"I'll apologize to her. I certainly didn't mean to hurt her feelings. But, Dad…" And Skylar looked at him again then, and didn't hide her frown. "I'm not sorry for what I said. I have a new life to figure out and there's no committee. I'm the one who has to do it."

Alone, a voice inside whispered.

And that was the thing, wasn't it? She'd had a shared life and she'd lost it. Of course it wasn't going to be pretty figuring out a way to move forward. It had been one thing to be single way back when. She hadn't known what she was missing; she'd only had ideas about it in the abstract. Now she knew.

The comfort and responsibility of a person always on her team and invested in her life. The voice on the other end of her first call. The shared language of jokes and fights, intimacy and sex, disappointments and dreams, spinning across years. Housekeeping skirmishes and roommate battles and golden evenings lit from within with private laughter no one else would ever understand. The difference between missing him in a home he'd return to and the finality of knowing that the emptiness there was permanent.

Now she knew exactly what she was missing.

"People care about you," Billy said, reminding her where she was.

"And I'm grateful." Skylar lifted her chin. "But that doesn't come with a vote on how I handle this."

"That's fine," Billy retorted. "No vote." The announcers

were talking again and the chute nearest them opened to a big round of applause, but he kept his gaze hard on her. "But stop kidding yourself, Skylar."

"I don't think I am."

"Believe me, I understand the appeal of a fling to shake things up, but it doesn't change anything. You're still you on the other side of it. The same problems as before you started. A fling doesn't do anything but complicate things."

Her tongue hurt and she realized she was literally biting it. "Noted."

"And you're not the type," he continued doggedly. He raised a hand when she scowled at him. "You grew up watching me make a fool of myself and I know exactly why you picked a good guy and settled down with him. Your sister did the same thing. You both held on to the first relationship you found because you watched me throw so many away. You think I don't know what that's a reaction to?"

"Scottie is perfectly happy with someone else," Skylar said tightly. Scottie was more than merely happy and her ex Alexander had been a cheating slime, but that was neither here nor there. "And not everything that happens in the world is about you."

"You never dated much before Thayer and he was a good one, Skylar. And the point is, you're not prepared. You're playing games without knowing the rules." It took her a minute to place the look in her father's eyes then and when she did, she froze. Because it was pity. *Pity.* She didn't know if she wanted to throw up or punch him, and he was still talking. "Men are dogs, sweetheart. Especially famous ones. You're going to get hurt."

And then the crowd around them was chanting, as if they'd heard the entire conversation. As if they agreed that Skylar was an idiot. As if everyone in the entire world knew what an idiot she was.

Cody. Cody.

But no, she realized when her heart receded a bit from taking over her throat, it was just because Cody was finally in the chute.

Which was good, because her father thought she was an idiot and it gave her an opportunity to talk herself down from stabbing him in the neck with the nearest sharp object. While making sure she didn't give in to the emotion pricking at the back of her eyes, because she would rather die than give him the satisfaction of thinking he'd scored a hit.

Cody. Cody.

Inside the chute, maybe ten feet away, she saw Cody nod to indicate he was ready.

She sucked in her breath as the gate flew open, and then Cody was there before her, high up on a mean old bull who looked particularly pissed off as he hurled himself out into the arena.

Skylar forgot her father had been talking to her. She forgot the whispers, the muttering. She forgot her walk of shame and this deeply appalling new trend that her romantic life was anyone else's concern but hers. Or that her own father thought she was some starry-eyed groupie, unable to discern a man's real intentions.

It all disappeared into the spectacle right there in front of her.

The bull spun, bucking wildly, but Cody was nothing but grace. Grace and control, his left hand high and his right clamped tight in his rope. The seconds spun out on the clock, the crowd getting louder with each jolt and jump.

More and more—everyone on their feet—and then the buzzer rang.

And Cody dismounted, hitting the ground and rolling while the bull fighters ran in to distract the bull. Cody rolled straight back up to his feet, taking off his hat to wave at the crowd—but the hat wave pissed the bull off.

He charged toward Cody, sending the bull fighters scattering.

And Cody jumped for the rails that separated the dirt arena from the stands, three rows below where Skylar was standing and watching him, her hands over her mouth and her heart a mad drumming in her chest.

The announcer called out the score—a high, much-deserved 89—and the bull was gradually coerced back into the chutes. Cody stayed up on the rails, waving his hat at the crowd again as they cheered on the score that put him in the lead, but his hard green gaze landed on Skylar.

It was only a second. A brief, electric moment across a crowd.

Cody's mouth crooked in the corner, and that was all it took.

It was as good as an engraved invitation, as far as Skylar was concerned. She knew in that blistering instant exactly where she was going to be tonight. And maybe for the rest of the weekend.

And her father was mistaken. This wasn't a game. Maybe it was a compulsion, but so what if it was? There were worse things.

She'd lived through one of them.

He jumped back down and walked out of the arena. Skylar stayed where she was, next to a father who thought she was a fool and more than a little loose besides, and she realized something she'd been shying away from all day because it didn't slot in nicely with her own image of herself.

No one had been more invested in her perfect show of grief than Skylar had been herself. And that meant more than simply being everybody's favorite shrine, it meant the endless patience and the widow's smile and accepting so many platitudes she wanted to scream.

Yet she hadn't. Until this morning.

Life wasn't a decorous funeral service, she thought as the crowd cheered around her and another bull tried to dislodge its rider by any means necessary. Life wasn't careful flower arrangements and the unctuous murmurings of funeral directors and distant uncles who barely knew the deceased. Life was ugly and messy and chaotic. It was complicated. It was too big to be squashed down into *should haves.*

Cody Galen was rough and hard and likely no good for her at all. And yet he made her feel after so many years frozen solid. He made her *feel.* Ugly and messy and chaotic and *good.*

So good she would do absolutely anything to keep right on feeling it as long as he was here and wanted her.

So good she didn't care what anybody else thought about it, or even if they thought she was an idiot.

So good that Skylar forgot to feel guilty that she was the one who'd lived.

Chapter Eight

CODY LIKED TO win.

He liked winning. He liked whiskey. He liked women.

Usually one led into the next, a celebratory slide into sin he greatly enjoyed partaking of along the endless road trip that was life on tour.

But for some reason, Skylar alone seemed to take the place of his usual variety pack, and he liked that too.

More than liked it.

Friday night, after he'd rode a sweet 89 like it was nothing and put himself in the lead, he'd seen her up there in the stands. And that was new. Not happening to recognize a woman he'd been with, but actually finding her and liking it when he did. Like she was some kind of touchstone.

The truth was, he'd never felt anything like that before.

His mother had certainly never wasted her time watching her only son try to kill himself riding bulls. Growing up, she'd acted like it was a phase he was going through. When he'd turned eighteen and joined the tour, she'd assured him that he'd end up crippled like all the bull riders she'd ever heard of—a friend of a friend's cousin twice removed or any old cowboy telling lies in a dive bar—and more, that she'd wash her hands of him if he did because she already had enough on her plate with Todd and the girls.

Cody had taken that as a clear indication that he was not a man who needed to stock the stands with friendly faces. And these days he took it as a point of pride that he was so solitary. He didn't cart family and friends around with him, much less girlfriends or pretty pieces of tail. And not only because he didn't do girlfriends. He didn't need it, he would have said. Better the stands were empty and he still won, because he was making his mark. He wanted to go down in history, not show off for a girl.

And anyway, friendly faces were lies. He knew what happened when friendly faces turned vicious, as soon as the door was closed and nobody else could see. More than one person had told him he had trust issues, of course. He preferred to think of it as straight-up practicality.

But there was no denying the fact that he liked looking up from the dirt in Billings to see Skylar's blue eyes open wide and filled with something that looked a whole lot like pride as they slapped to his.

Cody would have said that the back of a bull was the only thing in the world that could silence the crowd and make him forget where he was. That sweet, brutal dance he'd been doing so well for all these years. He would have said that was the only possible way to shut off his head and make everything in him go still and right.

But it turned out that maybe Skylar had the same kind of magic in her.

"Maybe I should get your number," he told her in a low, teasing kind of way, later that night.

She'd been waiting for him outside the arena. Out there by his truck, looking cuter than any woman should have the right to in jeans that were plastered all over her butt and pretty little cowboy boots as befitted a country girl. He been particularly taken by the little tank top she wore, as if she'd dressed to make him as hard as possible, with the delicate gold necklace around her neck and tiny little pearl nestled right there in her throat. Right where he most wanted to put his mouth.

All that and her crooked smile too.

If it wasn't magic, he didn't know what the hell it was.

He hadn't said a word when he'd seen her waiting for him, leaning against his bumper with her head tipped back like she was counting stars again. Like she could stand there all night and whether or not he showed up was incidental. Maybe that was Skylar's secret—she was the least needy female he'd ever encountered.

Which made him feel a little too close to needy for comfort.

It took one look at her for all the aches and pains that had swamped him in the locker room—the way they always did in the wake of all that adrenaline—to disappear. He kept coming, then picked her up, taking her mouth as she wrapped herself around him.

He kissed her until he thought he might get arrested, and then he tossed her in the cab of his truck.

And he barely made it to the city limits before he pulled the car over to some out-of-the-way park, and pulled her over him in the front seat. Because he couldn't wait another minute, much less the rest of the drive out to his Airstream.

It was possible he'd expected it to be a little less wild after the previous night. After all, he'd pretty much glutted himself on her.

But it had been more of the same.

Hot. Frenzied. Insane.

He figured it would be worth whatever fine he'd have to pay if they got caught.

"I don't give out my number," she breathed when that first storm passed, and they'd steamed up all his windows. She'd grinned at him, as if he wasn't still inside of her. As if he was some douchebag in a bar trying to buy a pretty girl a drink. "But I'll take yours."

Cody couldn't get enough of her.

Saturday had been the usual nonsense on a tour weekend. Because he was involved in local sponsorship, he had to show up and play the smiling, genial buffoon at the Grey Sports flagship store in downtown. He sat at the table with a couple of the other riders, and did his best to look approachable while dressed in the clothes they'd laid out for him.

"We're so happy to have a legend like you here today," the manager gushed at him as she led him to the table where he was expected to sit and sign autographs for a few hours.

But Cody noticed Skylar's father wasn't around to share that sentiment. He couldn't blame the man.

All he really wanted to do was stand up and stop pretending to be the gentleman cowboy he'd never been. He'd wanted to stop all the fake grinning into cameras with every kid and giggly woman who approached him. He wanted to stop shaking hands with men who were all belly and listening to them tell him lies about how they'd almost done a little bull riding themselves and maybe would again, if they could find a spare weekend.

He'd never liked the glad-handing and ass-kissing, but it seemed worse this time. Or maybe it was because he knew that Skylar was in the same store, if out of sight. And it was the same thing that kept happening to him. If he knew she was around, he had to have her.

"I'm working," she told him with mock severity when he found her, after his meet and greet was done. She was back in the offices, hunched over a pile of invoices, but he'd seen the way her eyes lit up when he walked in. "I'm very busy handling an inventory situation."

"I'm good at handling things," he told her. "Like locked doors."

And he'd showed her what he meant, right there against the door with the bolt thrown.

"I really should get your number," he murmured against the side of her face when they were done, and Skylar was flushed with that bright red that made him hard all over again.

She busied herself with her clothes, stepping away from him to right her blouse and button up her jeans, then run her palms over her smooth hair.

"Why do you need my number?" she asked. She snuck a bright look his way. "You seem to find me without it."

"Maybe I don't want to feel like a detective all the time."

That crooked smile made his chest feel tight, and the craziest part was, he was starting to get used to it.

"Detective looks good on you," she said. "You should keep it up."

"It's like you want me insecure, darlin'."

She laughed at that. At him, when no one ever did. And he liked that, too.

"I'm pretty sure you can handle it," she said.

Saturday was the big night, and Cody never let anything mess with his concentration. Not even the most fascinating woman he'd ever encountered. He shoved it aside and focused on his job.

His only job: riding the best bull he could to the most spectacular finish possible.

Cody drafted a particularly rank bull and then had to wait for his turn. He watched some of the other riders score a little too high for his liking, because he wanted that top slot.

He could taste it. By the time his bull was herded into the chutes, he was floating along in that strange, tight little bubble between anticipation and excitement that always heralded a big night.

He knew from experience that he couldn't let himself go too far one way or the other. And the only way to handle it was to concentrate on the tiny little details that made each ride work. Stepping up to the chute. Positioning himself right as he went in, and working on getting his rope nice and sticky and exactly where he wanted it. It was all about the rope, and every time he wanted to kick himself for a ride that hadn't come off the way he wanted it was because he hadn't paid enough attention to the rope when he'd had the opportunity.

He didn't make that mistake tonight. He took his time. The bull beneath him was feisty, jumping and rolling and having a little tantrum, just to show Cody what was in store. But that was what he wanted. Spirit and grit. And that wildness that nothing and no one could tame.

It was what made a bull a legend.

And it was what made a woman like Skylar magic.

Cody was more than ready for both. When the rope was right and he felt that little kick inside him, telling him it was time to get it done, he nodded—and that was it.

The gate opened and the flight began.

No thought.

No worry.

Just the dance.

All the training, all the strategy, the stress and the hope and the worry; all his years of practice and preparation, sacrifice and will, down to these few seconds.

One man, one beast.

One test of will.

It was amazing how the time slowed. Sometimes Cody worried it wouldn't, that it was over and *this* would be the ride that felt like a sick and terrifying blur, because that would be the end. That would be his last ride.

But it wasn't tonight.

Eight seconds were still a lifetime.

Time flattened out and ran sweet. What seemed like nothing but wild jolting and bucking, too wild to ever be conquered in any way, felt different here. Inside the bubble where it was him and the bull and the way they reacted to each other, feeding off one another, anticipating each other's game.

He felt how the bull moved and rolled with it. Away from his right hand that gripped on tight. He could feel when his left arm strayed too close to the bull's back and adjusted in that split second.

He had all the time in the world when he was in the zone. No crowd. No noise. No clock. No problem.

There was only the roll. The ride.

And just about when he thought that he could keep on doing it forever, the buzzer rang.

Another eight seconds down.

And time sped up again.

Cody worked his hand free, then took his jump from the bull's broad back to the ground, letting gravity take him into another roll in the dirt. His senses were so heightened that he swore he could feel where the bull fighters were without having to see them, as they raced in to distract the snorting bull while Cody found his feet.

This was the part Cody liked best. The rush. The sheer joy of having done it one more time, eight seconds and no pain.

It was this moment where it was all his. No score, no money won or lost, no reaction from the fans. It was just *his,* that ride he could feel in his bones like a wicked drug and the sheer thrill of it that all these years later he still hadn't gotten over.

It was this moment where he thought that maybe he never would.

But this time when he stood up, he was looking for a face in the crowd.

He wanted to hate himself for that kind of weakness, the exact sort of weakness he'd spent his life avoiding, but he couldn't. He just couldn't. Because there she was, just where he'd expected her a few rows up from the dirt, and he couldn't deny the jolt that went through him at the sight.

Not only couldn't he deny it, he liked it.

He felt Skylar all over. His head. His throat. His chest

and gut. His cock. Even his damned feet.

Head to toe and back again, and for another wild second that flattened out a little bit and sat heavy on him, the only thing he could see was the punch of her blue eyes from twenty feet away.

There was something about her that could ruin a man, he thought. Not only that, make him like it.

But then the announcer was belting out his score, another 89, which meant Cody was holding on to his lead. The crowd went wild. Cody doffed his hat the way he always did, and took his moment to bask in the applause.

Even if, when he made his way out of the arena to do the usual interviews, the only thing he really remembered was Skylar. Watching him as if there was no one in the arena but the two of them.

His second ride of the night was wilder. A newer bull out to prove he was a badass, and Cody equally determined to show him who was the real boss, to the tune of an even higher 89, just shy of a legendary 90.

Which meant Cody won the weekend.

He stood in the center of the ring and he waved as everyone cheered and he didn't think about the money, for a change. He didn't think about how to allocate it and where he should send it or count up how much time he had left in this.

For the first time in years, he relaxed and enjoyed the moment. The cheers. The rush.

The knowledge that she was out there.

And instead of his usual form of celebration, which generally ranked high in the debauchery stakes and involved enough whiskey to regret it all the next morning, it turned out all he wanted was the woman waiting for him out at his truck again. As if they planned it.

As if she'd read his mind.

"I guess I don't need your number after all," he drawled as he walked toward her. "Since you seem to be stalking me."

"Oh, I might actually give it to you now," she told him, her blue eyes dancing with that laughter he couldn't seem to stop craving, half in and half out of the shadows. "I like a winner. Isn't that the buckle bunny way?"

"It's less of a philosophy and more of an act. Or a series of actions, to be more precise."

"By all means. Let's make sure we're precise. About the groupies."

"Precision is my life, darlin'."

He drew closer. He eyed her there on his bumper but kept going. He beeped open the truck, threw his gear inside. But he kept his eyes on Skylar while he did it.

"But if you think about it, there's got to be some kind of hierarchy," she was saying, in a musing sort of voice as if she really had given the matter a lot of thought.

She didn't stop talking when he roamed back over in her direction and planted himself directly in front of her. Maybe a little too close, come to that. He saw her pulse go a little crazy in her neck, but she didn't otherwise react.

"Hierarchical bunnies?" he asked.

Well. It was more of a drawl, more smoke than laughter.

She shivered slightly, but kept on. "You know. Which bunnies think they deserve the higher ranked riders versus which bunnies will take any old cowboy just to say they're in the game."

"You know a lot about the inner workings of buckle bunnies, do you?"

"Not as such." She let out a little laugh, breathy and sweet, when he reached over and hooked two fingers in the waistband of her jeans to haul her toward him. Better yet, she went to him like butter. "But I do know about groups of girls. Not sure it's ever really all that different. Where to sit in the cafeteria during the worst part of seventh grade or the adventures of the American Extreme Bull Riders Tour buckle bunny crew. I think there's probably some overlap."

"Next time I see a bunny hopping around I'll have to ask about seventh grade," Cody murmured, his face near hers, so he could feel it when she let out one of those jagged breaths.

He didn't kiss her.

He reveled in the crispness of the way she felt, out here in another endless Montana night. How soft her skin was against the backs of his fingers, there where they brushed against her belly. That scent she wore that drove him crazy, cedar and summer and Skylar.

And whatever the hell it was that drew him to her this

way, filling up his head and making him hard. Flattening out time like he was on a different kind of ride, making him look for her blue gaze in a stadium filled with people chanting his name.

He'd only seen her.

"The truth is," he told her, as if he was whispering the kind of sweet poetry he'd never uttered in his life, "I've never known a bunny to overlook an opportunity to talk about herself."

She was melting against him, her arms looped around his neck so she could hold on, and he knew her now. He knew the way her cute little body worked. Last night he'd had her in his truck, but that had only been the start. When they'd finished, he'd kept on driving them out into the darkness until they'd reached his Airstream, and they'd both been laughing as if they'd shared a whole bottle of whiskey on the way as they made their way inside.

That was what this woman did to him. She made him feel drunk when he wasn't.

He'd learned a whole lot about Skylar in his narrow little shower. He'd learned that she was stubborn. Determined. That when she got something in her head, she kept right on until she did it.

And what she'd wanted to do was wash every part of him. First with soap and water. Then with her mouth.

"What are you doing?" he'd asked when she inched down his front, making noises he couldn't quite interpret in the back of her throat as she first cleaned him off, then trailed fire over him with every lick of her tongue or touch of her lips.

"I'm tracking all the scars and bruises," she'd said. "I want to make sure I get each one."

But she didn't say it the way a few women had in the past, in a weird little baby voice as if they were playing nurse.

Skylar said it softly. With great certainty. As if she thought they were beautiful.

As if she thought he was.

She washed every part of him, thoroughly, and then she knelt down before him in what little space there was and proceeded to show him exactly how beautiful she thought he was. She took him in deep. She used her mouth and her hands, bringing him to a loud, shouting finish—so intense he'd almost punched his fist through the wall of his own trailer.

And then it had been his turn. He'd soaped her up and he'd washed her down, reveling in the slippery feel of all her tight little curves in his hands. Then he'd carried her out to his bed, laying her out and settling over her so he could take his time with her.

Again. And again.

But it didn't seem to matter how often he glutted himself on her. He still wanted more.

"I think there's some kind of party," she whispered now.

She brought him back to the stadium. Billings. The

money he'd just won and what that meant for his half-sisters. And him. And the fact that he hadn't really thought too much about either.

"I'm not a big partier," he told her. He moved his hands up and down her back, reminding himself how well she fit him. How much he craved her, again, as if he hadn't helped himself to all this goodness earlier today, up against the door in that office. "You want me to take you out, Skylar? You want to go on a date?"

Cody realized once he said it that he expected it to piss her off. And more, that he was surprised he hadn't done it already. He wasn't a nice man. He didn't pretend to be. And he usually made sure to disabuse a woman of any notion that there was something more between them than his dick—usually halfway through getting laid in the first place.

He'd already neglected to make it clear where things lay with Skylar. Maybe that was why he couldn't figure it out himself, which was unacceptable.

But she didn't get pissed. She moved her hands so she could prop them against his pectoral muscles, and then she gazed at him solemnly.

"Is that a euphemism?"

He considered. "I don't think so."

"Maybe we should skip the date part and go straight to the end of the night part. Because between you and me, I think I like that part better than sitting around in nice clothes pretending to be well behaved."

"I am shocked and appalled," he drawled. "I think you might be getting the wrong idea about me. I'm not just a pretty face, Skylar. I have a brain too."

She let out a sound that it took him a minute to realize was a full-on giggle. A little high-pitched and entirely too cute.

If she'd taken out a dagger and stabbed him, he doubted he would have felt it any less. Like a shot straight between his ribs.

"That sounds like something a buckle bunny would say," she said when she stopped giggling. "Are you a buckle bunny, Cody?"

"Buckle bunnies don't talk that much, darlin'. I think you're missing the entire point of buckle bunnies."

"You're the one who wants to go on a date. You know that it's generally a public activity, right? You have to keep all your clothes on your body and your hands more or less to yourself. Pretty much the exact opposite of anything we've ever done together."

"I'm getting the distinct impression you're only in this for my body," Cody said, sorrowfully.

"More what you can do with it."

"You're a shallow woman."

But he kissed her then. Deep. Hot. As if they were already naked. As if he was already so deep inside her, she'd started making that little keening sound in the back of her throat that told him she was close to coming.

Just thinking about it made his cock ache.

He picked her up and put her in the truck on the driver's side, mostly so he could keep his hands on her a while longer. And when he swung in beside her, she hadn't moved over all that far on the bench seat, so he hooked his hand over the curve of her thigh and held it there a minute.

Held them both there until he heard that little sigh she made when she was totally relaxed.

And this was the time to end things. Cody knew that.

He didn't spend consecutive nights with women because he'd always worried that it would get to exactly this place. He knew her too well. They were joking around instead of getting straight to the good stuff. It already felt a hell of a lot more intimate than anything he'd ever wanted.

He'd always thought that he didn't want to get here because he would find it boring. He liked sex, not conversation. It had never occurred to him that it would be just the opposite. That the more he knew about Skylar, the more he wanted to know. But that surprising fact didn't change anything.

He was a man who lived on the road. A new city every weekend, and he'd seen what a toll that took on all the riders around him. He'd seen broken marriages, pissed-off kids, and how exhausted the men were when they tried to race home for a couple of days every week only to head back out for a new show every weekend. He'd seen the cheating, the divorces, and the toll all that took on each cowboy's performance. Cody had never wanted any part of that. He took himself from city to city, and the only baggage he brought with him was what he could fit in his Airstream.

He needed to cut this off. Because tomorrow he needed to get on the road and start heading west toward Missoula, where next week's show took place.

"Skylar," he began.

And she didn't tense up at the serious note in his voice. There was no sudden spike of anxiety in the cab of the truck. He had his hand on her leg and he could feel that she didn't so much as breathe heavy.

Not Skylar. She shifted so she could look at him, that lopsided smile on her lips, and waited.

Just waited.

And he'd said some version of this a million times. *Don't get too attached. I don't want to lead you on. It's not you, darlin', it's me.* All that same old cowboy shit.

All of it was true. And necessary to get out there, so there were no expectations or recriminations later when he drove away the way he always did. Without a single regret or glance in the rearview mirror.

So he didn't know why he was having such trouble opening up his mouth and saying it now.

Maybe it was because if she wanted anything from him, she sure didn't show it. He hadn't called her. She hadn't complained about it. He'd joked about getting her number, but she hadn't written it down. Or snuck it into his jeans pocket. Or straight-up written it on his hand.

Every time they parted, she kissed him, smiled at him, and then walked away.

Cody had the sinking realization that Skylar might not actually require any letting down easy. That she might be the first woman he'd ever met who didn't want more from him than he could give.

It should have made him jubilant. So he had no idea why it just irritated the hell out of him instead.

"What are you doing next weekend?" he asked.

He actually asked her that and was so appalled by the fact it had come out of his mouth that he sat there, something like winded.

"Oh, you mean because the rodeo won't be in town?" She laughed at that, apparently unaware that he was losing it beside her. "That's a good question. What do buckle bunnies do when there are no buckles around?"

"This is Montana." And maybe his tone was a little too dark. "There's always another cowboy."

When she was quiet beside him for a moment he thought he'd finally managed to get to her. And then wondered what the hell was wrong with him that pissing her off was something he even wanted. And worse, why he didn't like doing it, when he'd never minded one way or the other before.

Because before it was never Skylar, a voice inside him piped up.

"If you want my number that badly, Cody, you can just ask for it." Her voice was even. Her gaze was steady. And he felt like he was ripping apart from the inside out. "And if you don't, that's perfectly okay too. A whole lot of people seem to be under the impression that I don't know what this is. But let me assure you, I do."

If she was actively trying to piss *him* off, she couldn't have picked a better way to do it. Because if he didn't know what this was, how the hell could she?

"Do you?" He tried to take the crazy out of his voice. With limited success. "What is it?"

"I'll assume that's a little test. Don't worry, I've always been really good at tests." She shifted beside him, straightening up in her seat as if she was mimicking some kind of perfect pupil. "You don't have to tell me that you're a commitment phobic cowboy, Cody. That's pretty obvious. It goes with the laconic thing. And all that swagger. And the good news is, a commitment phobic cowboy is pretty much exactly what the doctor ordered."

"Perfect. Now I'm a prescription."

"Better than Xanax," she said brightly. And the craziest part was that she was smiling. Actually smiling. "You don't have to worry about me. I'm not going to get the wrong idea. I'm not going to freak out. I don't want more than you can give and there's definitely no need for any emotional scenes. What you see with me is exactly what you get."

"Bullshit."

He didn't know where that came from. But he didn't take it back.

She only raised her eyebrows. "Okay. Don't believe me. I can call a taxi right now, you know. We don't even have to have this conversation."

"Here's the thing." Cody shifted around on the seat so he could look at her a little more closely, and then he hooked a hand over the nape of her neck. Just so he could pull her in a little further. Because he wanted her so close it was almost a kiss. Because he wanted her to feel all the things that he felt. And maybe also because he was a dick. "I've scraped off so many women I don't even know their names."

"How charming."

"I'm not bragging. It's a fact. I've had this conversation a thousand times."

"And there's absolutely no need for this to be a thousand and one."

"I'm tired," he told her. Starkly and without any flourish. "In bull-riding terms I might as well be the crypt keeper. That's how old I am. And I'm tired of everything. The tour. Living on the road. The hustle of it all. I've been over for it for a long time."

"That's no way to live."

That was all she said, and then seemed content to sit there in the dark of the truck. And Cody didn't know what it was about this woman. He didn't understand why nothing seemed to get to her. Why all she did was gaze back at him, calm and easy.

Or why the fact she kept doing it made him…somebody he didn't recognize.

Someone chatty.

"All I have are eight seconds on a bull," he told her, because apparently this was who he was now. A guy who never shut his mouth. "Eight seconds where none of the rest of this crap matters. Whether I'm old, whether I'm young, whether the next fall will cripple me—it doesn't matter. I get eight seconds of glory, that's all."

"That's more than some people ever get," she said quietly, as if she knew.

And he was still a total stranger to himself, because he kept going.

"There's only one thing that feels anything like those eight seconds, Skylar. One thing, and I've tried a thousand." He pulled her face another inch closer. "You."

He couldn't really believe he'd said that out loud. And from the stunned look on her face, neither could she.

But the craziest part was that it was true. He didn't know why he hadn't realized it the first time he'd seen her, standing at her father's front door with ghosts in those blue eyes of hers.

"I'm not making any declarations," he told her gruffly, ignoring the fact he already had, whether he wanted to admit that or not. "I'm not that guy. I'm never going to be that guy. But I'm not ready to be done with you."

Her lips moved into that lopsided little tilt that wedged its way deep into him. Again.

"Be still my heart."

Cody wanted to be inside of her. He should have waited until he was to have this conversation he hadn't known he planned to have. He needed to be deep inside her because that was where everything made sense. More than made sense, it was *right.*

But even the thought of it soothed him a little bit. It took the edge off. It made him imagine that he hadn't just said the most insane thing he could possibly have said. Out loud.

To her.

"You got something to do next weekend?" he asked her.

This time with a little more intensity.

"As a matter of fact, my schedule is wide open."

And her voice wasn't calm anymore. There was that hitch in it. Just like the ghosts in her eyes that told him she wasn't nearly as calm or controlled as she pretended she was. Somehow that soothed him too.

Cody shifted his hand from the back of her neck to the sweet little V of her T-shirt. And he played with the hem, tracing it up one side and then down the other until he got that shiver he was after.

"I'm going to be in Missoula," he told her, as if it was the kind of sweet shit he didn't know how to say. "Tomorrow I'm going to hitch up the Airstream and head west. I'll probably take my time. I like to see a little bit of the country while I'm out here on tour. Or the years disappear without my really noticing it."

"That sounds like an excellent plan."

"That's not a plan, that's my routine. Same old, same old." He traced that V again. Up, then down. Then once more. "Skylar. Come with me."

And everything in him froze. He was intent and still and poised there on a knife's edge as she stared back at him.

She made him wish he was the kind of man who could pull out a poem and make it work. But the only poetry he'd ever known was the hard work of a sweet ride, and he'd asked her to come with him. He didn't have anything but that.

"Cody," she said, using his name the same way he'd used hers. Serious. Somber.

He thought she was going to say no, and that was another moment that went on for a lifetime, telling him things about himself he didn't really want to know.

But then she smiled. And leaned in close.

And whispered her number in his ear.

Chapter Nine

EVERY DAY THERE was a parade of *deep concern* into every inbox Skylar had.

Family and friends alike felt the need to weigh in about her decision to hit the road with Cody, in varying degrees of ALL CAPS astonishment. Every person Skylar knew thought she'd lost her mind, which didn't have the result they all clearly wanted.

She didn't take the next flight home. She settled in a little more with Cody instead.

I'm sure the man is hot, Scottie texted. *And hot is great. But are you really the person who runs away with the rodeo? That doesn't sound like you.*

Skylar got that particular text from her sister a day or so after she'd packed a bag and left Billings. There had been no further scenes with her father or Angelique. They'd been out with the kids when she'd swung by that Sunday morning, so she'd had the great pleasure of writing them a note and avoiding the drama altogether.

If that was cowardly, she was at peace with it.

"Did you really leave me a note?" Billy demanded on her voicemail that same night, all the usual bluster and that darker current underneath that she thought might be hurt feelings. It made her feel something like small inside—but not enough to return his call. "A *note,* Skylar? You really made Angelique feel bad. I hope you're proud."

And it was the irony of that Skylar found she savored most as Cody had driven them west across Montana's eastern plains, then up over the brash jut of Rockies. Because her father seemed to have forgotten his own long history of leaving notes to handle situations he didn't want to deal with, like the fact he'd wanted a divorce from Skylar's mother. Carolyn had left that particular note on the refrigerator, held fast by a magnet they'd gotten on a bitter family trip to Kansas, until Scottie had ripped it up and thrown it in the fire during one of the unpleasant mid-divorce winters.

But if Billy didn't know how ridiculous his outrage sounded, Skylar wasn't about to clue him in. Because that would require calling him back and opening herself up for all manner of commentary she didn't want. She opted for a quick text instead.

Will be in touch soon. Love to all.

Scottie's text had come late the next day, suggesting to Skylar that there had been a lot of unusual family discussion about her.

Apparently I'm exactly that person, she'd texted Scottie. *I'm as surprised as you are.*

Cody had bypassed Missoula, heading north to find a perfect little spot near the vastness of Flathead Lake to spend the time before the weekend show. Skylar hadn't been to the lake since a trip in junior high school, if she was remembering correctly, but nothing had changed. She caught her breath in the same awe she recalled from back when as Cody drove them up and over the hills to the south. Flathead Lake gleamed blue and impossible before them, so big and wide it seemed like a dream, while the Mission Mountains stood sentry to the east. It was jaw-dropping. It made Skylar's Montanan heart beat a little faster.

It made her think there was nothing better in the world than finding a place where they could spend a few days, nestled in the pine trees down by the water's edge, as if the rest of the planet ceased to exist. Just for a little while.

Though no one in her life wanted to let her go off and do that.

Everyone, apparently, was an expert on exactly what kind of person Skylar was. And exactly what she should do. And more to the point, what she absolutely should not do in the company of a bad-boy bull rider, because she would regret it later. Or because it was as out of character as a drug binge and more scary, because she wasn't actually high. Or because her behavior somehow tarnished Thayer's memory, half a country away from the life she'd lived with him and his place in his family's vault.

You will hate yourself for this, one of her Atlanta friends told her very seriously in an email of several dense paragraphs. The same friend who had spent years cheating on her sweet, emotionally available boyfriend with her awful, aloof musician ex. *You will feel dirty forever.*

It took everything Skylar had not to respond: *I think maybe you're talking about you, not me.*

There were a whole lot of consequences waiting out there for her, Skylar noted every time a new text or email or voicemail came in, and everyone could not only see them coming at her, but really—*really*—wanted to make sure she knew all about them in advance. Because they were all deeply worried that, somehow, she might have overlooked the complexities of her own life. Or forgotten who she was. Or let Cody knock her over the head and drag her off by her hair into his den of iniquity.

What no one ever bothered to ask was how Skylar actually felt about what she was doing. Or the man she was doing it with.

And she was grateful for that, she thought now, sitting on the steps of the Airstream with her feet in the grass. Pine trees towered overhead and the July morning was still cool, with hints of the heat to come later on. The Mission Mountains turned different colors in the light, rising there on the other side of the sparkling, dancing water. And out there in front of her, cutting a fine form through all that golden-tipped blue, was Cody.

This was the "little swim" he liked to take after he did his usual routine of intense resistance training and then ran a few miles. Sometimes Skylar joined him for part of the run, but there was no keeping up with him. She liked to try, but always ended up laughing and waving him off before turning and walking back to their sweet little camp.

Before Cody, she'd never really thought of bull riders as athletes. They were usually hot in that laconic cowboy way, sure, but she'd never considered them the same as, say, football players. Maybe she'd thought that they simply climbed atop bulls and held on tight, which seemed more a question of grip and less about skill or athleticism.

She'd learned otherwise.

Cody came by the stamina she'd experienced in his bedroom—and in his truck, and out beneath the Montana sky, and in the office of Grey Sports—honestly. And he dedicated himself to honing it all the time. He not only worked out daily, he had a great many opinions about food and what he would and would not put in the body he treated like a favorite machine.

"I thought you liked to throw back the whiskey and get your party on," she'd said when the true breadth of his *my body is a temple* mindset became clear to her.

Cody had grinned at her as he prepared something else green. "Whiskey is for winning. Everything else is training."

For a woman who'd spent years in the Deep South, where bacon grease was considered its own kind of holy water, it was an adjustment.

Skylar smiled a little as she let the grass tickle the bottoms of her feet. Despite the food and exercise and athleticism thing, which was all a surprise, what was most surprising about living with a man she hardly knew in a sleek, compact trailer was how easy it was.

"I was worried we'd have nothing to talk about and would just have sex the whole time," she'd told him this morning on the part of his run she'd shared, already panting and out of breath after a few yards.

Cody, not at all out of breath, had laughed. "That was a worry? I thought that was the draw."

"I thought it could get old."

"Are we talking about the same thing?" He'd nudged her slightly with his arm as they'd run down the long, shaded dirt road that wound down into the forest, with gorgeous little views of the lake peeking at them from behind the trees. "I make you scream, woman. Every time. Show a little respect."

He was right. He did make her scream and she'd expected that part. It was all the rest of it that she hadn't been prepared for. The stories he told as they drove for hours across some of the most beautiful country in the world. That dry humor of his that popped out more often the more time they spent together. The simple pleasure of sitting across a table from him in the mornings as they both checked their various devices and caught up on news, both personal and global. She often slid her feet onto his lap. He often circled one of her ankles with his hand, absently, as if he was anchoring her to him.

Skylar knew there were words for the way that made her

feel, but she shoved all of that aside. None of this was about her heart. None of this was supposed to have that kind of depth or meaning. No resonance. This was nothing more and nothing less than what it seemed: a few days in the wilds of her beloved Montana with a man who wanted very specific things from her and no more.

What no one could seem to understand, sitting out there in judgment of her, was that Skylar had been displaced for two long years. It felt good to know exactly where she fit and what she was supposed to do. It felt more than good. She liked knowing the parameters. She liked knowing exactly what was happening, for a change.

It made her feel safe in a way she hadn't since before Thayer died.

Her phone buzzed beside her, alerting her to a new call, and she was surprised to see it was her brother. Surprised, then wary.

Because the last time Jesse had called her had been to question her decision to move to Billings. Three guesses what this call would be about.

She thought about letting it go to voicemail, but the man was getting married in a few short weeks and Skylar was a bridesmaid. There was always the possibility that he was calling about something related to her sisterly duties.

"I must be missing something," Jesse said by way of a greeting when Skylar picked up the call. Skylar could hear traffic sounds behind him, reminders that where he lived in big-city Seattle there were all the sorts of stores and museums and signs of urban life that she'd loved so much in Atlanta. And yet somehow didn't miss, sitting out here on a gorgeous summer morning with nothing but blue skies, green trees, mountains and water in every direction. "Maybe Dad had a stroke? Because he said something about you running off with the rodeo."

"When did we become phone-call people?" Skylar shifted on the Airstream's steps and let the sun dance over her face. "Because I could've sworn that we weren't that kind of family. And here we are again. On the phone. Discussing my life choices that you heard about through phone calls with our father, a man you have never taken as an authority on anything. Ever."

"I spend my entire day talking on the damn phone to people I don't want to talk to," her brother said. In that voice of his that was all business and was likely supposed to remind her that he was very important, but only made her roll her eyes. He might be the king of construction out in Seattle, marrying the ridiculously wealthy woman who was the right hand of Amos Burke, everybody's favorite computer genius, but he was just Jesse to Skylar. Her annoying older brother. "The last thing I wanted to do is any more of it. So that should tell you, Skylar, that your life choices are being treated as an emergency situation."

"There's no emergency. I'm perfectly fine. Feel free to report back."

"The rodeo, though? Really, cowgirl?"

"I shouldn't have to tell a man named after a famous Wild West outlaw, born and raised in Montana, the difference between a rodeo and the American Extreme Bull Riders."

"I have to tell you, this is a curve ball," he said after a moment and what she was pretty sure was a hastily concealed laugh. "I never figured you for the problem child. That was always me. And I figured if there was a dark horse who might come from behind to mess things up now that Dad and I are talking again, it would be Scottie. She's always had a little freak show in her soul."

There was no reason that should have pricked at Skylar. As if he was insulting her when she was almost certain that was meant to be a compliment.

"She's a corporate lawyer. It's basically the least freak show thing you could possibly do unless you became a tax attorney. Or possibly a pastor."

"I don't think you know about the secret lives of tax attorneys, Skylar. Or the average pastor, for that matter."

"Just like you don't know about the secret life of *me,* Jesse. Or anything else about me, apparently."

"You were the one who wanted a family," Jesse replied, a little too quick and much too certain for Skylar's liking. "Always. After all that bullshit between Mom and Dad, who could blame you for wanting something stable?"

She pinched the bridge of her nose and had the sense she

was willing back a headache. "Thank you for making me sound like a psychology textbook. Something I would have doubted you ever read, incidentally."

"You found a nice guy and you hung on," Jesse continued. "There's no shame in that. He was a good guy and he treated you right. He was everything Dad wasn't. If you'd searched the entire planet, you couldn't have found a guy less like Dad than Thayer."

Skylar tensed, waiting for the mention of Thayer to roll through her like a thunderstorm, but it didn't. She felt the same tug she always did. The memory of his face. His smile. His arms wrapping around her in that bear hug of his she'd always loved so much. But for the first time, thinking of him felt more sweet than bitter.

And then the fact that there was no storm made her feel as if she was sitting on the deck of a wildly pitching ship for a moment, surrendering to the waves whether she wanted to or not.

She had to dig her bare feet into the dirt to get her bearings. And some part of her wasn't sure she wanted to.

"All I'm saying is that this seems like a deliberate and calculated swing in the opposite direction," Jesse concluded. "Like maybe you're trying to scrub your past from your life by desecrating it a little bit."

"Desecrating it," she repeated. "Wow. I may not be acting exactly the way everyone expects me to act, but I have to tell you, that strikes me as everyone else's problem, not mine."

"It's just a theory."

There were so many things she wanted to say. Unkind things about Jesse's romantic past. Defenses. Arguments. But there was no point.

"You don't even know him," she pointed out quietly. "He could be a living saint."

"You're not the kind of girl who has flings, Skylar," Jesse replied. "Does he know that?"

"Do you?" she retorted.

And then she ended the call, because Cody was coming out of the water and she didn't want him to hear her. And more—Cody in swim trunks low on his hips and nothing else made her heart kick at her and her whole body go a little limp in anticipation.

Because being near him was always about anticipation.

"Rough call?" he asked as he drew close, rubbing a towel over his sculpted, scarred chest and making it all that much worse.

"My brother," she murmured, noncommittally, because she wanted to think about his acres of hard-packed perfection, gleaming with water—not Jesse.

Cody's dark green gaze was direct and burned its way into her whether she wanted it to or not.

"You don't have to tell me your stuff," he said, a little stiltedly, she thought. As if she was disappointing him, too. And she didn't know why that made her stomach knot up when no one else's disappointment seemed to touch her. "But don't pretend nothing's happening when I can see it all over your face."

"He's getting married soon," Skylar said shortly. "That's what's happening."

"And let me guess." Cody hung his towel around his neck. "I'm not his fantasy wedding date for his sister."

Skylar wanted to get up then, but she thought that if she did, he would see that he was getting to her and she couldn't allow that. She thought something in her might break wide open if she let him see how deep under her skin he was, because she might not have had a whole lot of flings, but she was pretty sure the whole point of them was to avoid depths of any kind.

"You're not good date material," she reminded him, throwing his own words back at him from the night they'd met. "You told me so yourself."

"You told me your family could use a little horrifying," Cody replied instantly, clearly not fazed at all. But Skylar was even more surprised that he clearly remembered that conversation they'd had out behind her father's house. "And it looks like I'm already doing my part. Why not eat some sad chicken at a big party filled with people who hate me? I'm hungry already."

"You don't want to go to a wedding." Skylar could hear that her voice was too raw, but she didn't know how to stop it. How to change it. How to back up somehow and get off this strange path she was on.

Something moved over Cody's face, then. Some shadow that Skylar told herself was the sun behind a cloud, nothing more.

And she didn't want to hear whatever he was about to say. She didn't want to allow this moment to get any weirder. There was a storm coming, she could feel it inside like that spooky wind that made her hair stand on end in the summertime, and it wasn't about Thayer.

It was about her.

It was about this.

And Skylar had always been a good girl. Jesse wasn't wrong about that. She'd not only never done something like this before, she'd always let *something like this* be something that other people started. Not her. Maybe she was happy to go along, but she'd never been much for the initiation.

She didn't really know how to go about it. It was one thing to roll with something that was already happening. It was something else to make it happen.

Skylar decided not to overthink it.

She stood up in a sudden surge, glad that she was wearing nothing but the little, stretchy sundress that could be worn as a top, a dress, or a skirt depending on her mood. She pulled it up and over her head, then dropped it to one side, and stood there in nothing but her thong.

Then, as Cody's gaze got dark and heated, she hooked her fingers in the sides of her panties and tugged them down her legs, kicking the little scrap away. And then she was standing there before him, completely naked, letting the Montana summer pour all over her. There was the sound of motorboats in the distance. Birds and waves against the shore. The rustle of the wind high up in the trees.

But all she could see was that arrested look on Cody's face. It made everything inside of her melt.

Then hum.

Cody dropped his towel and reached over to get his hands on her, making them both sigh a little when his palms closed over her hips. He brought his mouth down to hers but didn't kiss her, teasing them both.

Skylar surged up onto her toes, pressing as much of her body against his as she could, reveling in the feel of his skin, cooled from the lake, against hers. Her nipples ached into hard points. She felt wild and raw and slippery with need, as if she hadn't had him deep inside of her already this morning.

It was never enough. She always wanted more. And she didn't need anyone to tell her that didn't bode well. A fling was supposed to feel shallow. *She* was supposed to feel shallow.

But the things she felt when she touched this man were anything but.

"Maybe you have a point," Cody muttered, right there against her mouth, when Skylar couldn't remember that she'd been trying to make a point in the first place.

But then she didn't care, because he was picking her up and carrying her inside, where both of them could indulge the fire that burned so bright between them.

And Skylar could pretend that all of this was what it was supposed to be. Shallow. Temporary. Easy and fun.

Nothing raw. Nothing real.

Because this was just a fling, nothing more.

Chapter Ten

IT HAD NEVER occurred to Cody that the bulls might turn out to be the least of his concerns.

The second one he rode in Tacoma—a week after he made a little noise in Missoula because he'd always liked Montana—was particularly ornery. It threw him off at six spine-slamming seconds and to add insult to near-injury, he landed funny. Funny enough to trigger an old knee issue that he'd hoped he'd beaten this season—or at least beaten into submission after a few years of drama and shooting agony when he least expected it.

But no, there it was again, making the doctor who traveled with the tour mutter dire predictions over him when he went to get taped that Cody pretended he didn't hear. It also made him limp around like a man twice his age when he jumped off a bull, which got the rookies calling him *Grandpa* and the tour announcers opining about how much he had left in him at his advanced age.

All of that was annoying.

And yet it was still less irritating—less irritating, less fascinating, and definitely less wholly life-altering in ways he didn't really feel like examining too closely—than Skylar Grey.

He'd invited her to come with him to Missoula, and he couldn't say he'd really thought much beyond that. He hadn't considered what might happen in those slow, sweet days of sun and sex. He told himself that all he'd really been thinking about was the sex, but in his quieter moments, when it was just him and those truths he wanted most to ignore, he recognized that had never been about the sex, as good as it was.

It had been about Skylar. He hadn't wanted to let go.

And the crazy thing was, he still didn't.

They'd spent one week in Montana, and he'd been so fired up after Missoula that he'd asked her to stay with him another week. Another week of bright summer days in the high country, crossing over the Rockies as they made their way over the Lolo Pass out of Montana and into Idaho to follow the mighty Snake River a while. Then they'd picked their way across eastern Washington, skirting Mt. Rainier to make it into Tacoma in time for the next show.

And Cody wasn't bored, the way he'd always assumed he'd be if he spent too long with a woman. Or really anyone. Skylar pissed him off, but not because she was hard to live with. Or even to travel with.

Everything about her was easy. That was the problem. She hadn't caused any trouble in the stands when he'd comped her a ticket and got her a seat with the wives and families. There were a thousand ways for a new girl to get off on the wrong foot when she was thrown in with the fiercely loyal family sector, but Skylar charmed them all.

She was perfect. Except for the small, irritating little fact that she was resolutely determined that the whole damn thing between them was temporary.

It hadn't escaped Cody's notice that this was usually his position on these things. He was normally the one throwing down time limits and modifying expectations and ranting on about what was temporary and what wasn't. But that had changed for him right about the time he'd asked her to come with him the first time, and there didn't seem to be any chance of it changing back.

And he couldn't say he particularly enjoyed the shoe being on the other foot.

But what he enjoyed even less than that was the fact that he couldn't seem to get through to her.

She gave him her body. Night after night. And a whole lot of times during the day as well. Whenever and however he wanted her, she gave herself to him. And hell, she took, too. He thought that the day she'd stripped in front of him, out there in the open with Flathead Lake stretched out behind them like a silent, beautiful witness, was burned into his retinas and his mind and his unruly cock forever. And that hadn't been the only time she'd demanded a piece of him and taken it.

But it was always, only, sex.

She was driving Cody crazy.

The Sunday morning after failing to win anything in Tacoma—after he'd taken her hard and determined, as if he was trying to work out his frustrations right there on her luscious little body—she padded out from the Airstream's bedroom that he found entirely too easy to share with her to find him in the compact little living area, icing his damned knee.

"Is it still giving you a hard time?" she asked.

And she was killing him. Cody thought she was really, seriously killing him. She'd tossed on one of his T-shirts and it hung on her like a very short, much too intriguing little dress. He could see the outline of her breasts behind the soft fabric and the hem played tag with her upper thighs. And all he wanted to do was pull her close and get his hands up beneath it.

There was something about the way her hair looked all tousled in the mornings. There was something about that scratch in her voice and that faint fog in her blue eyes that made everything in him hum a little bit, as if she was the tuning fork and all he did was sing in her presence.

"It's not my knee that's pissing me off," he told her.

She blinked at him. Then smiled, which didn't exactly help anything.

"That sounds very cranky." But Skylar didn't get bent out of shape about things like his mood. She didn't take things personally. Cody kind of wished she would. "Do you need me to make you some coffee?"

"I saw that you packed," he said instead of saying yes, he would love some of that ridiculously good coffee she made.

And then he wished he could rip those words back and shove them back down his throat.

But he couldn't. So instead, he watched her go still. He watched the sleep fade from her eyes, making the blue of them look different, somehow. Wary.

"You going somewhere?" he asked, sounding like the jealous asshole he'd never been. Ever. In his entire life.

"Well, yes." She threaded her fingers together in front of her, which he knew by now meant that she was uncomfortable. But he had no sympathy for her when he'd never been so far from comfortable before. "I figured…"

She shrugged, but Cody knew what she figured. It was like every thought she had was stamped onto her forehead, scrolling past in capital letters he could read from a mile away, and it always came to the same conclusion. She always wanted to end this, whatever the hell it was. She always wanted it done.

And he…didn't.

Cody didn't bother to try to talk to her about whatever it was that was keeping her from settling in and enjoying whatever this was for as long as it lasted, the way he did. He knew better than to ask her about her feelings, God help him, or all those ghosts he knew she was running from, right there in her eyes. She didn't even want to talk about her brother's wedding, that she'd invited him to when he was a stranger and that she definitely didn't want him at now that he wasn't that anymore. Not quite that.

There was no getting close to Skylar. Anytime he tried, she closed up tight. Or tried to distract him from the subject at hand, and he was only a man. He let her.

"I have some land," he told her now.

His voice was low and he told himself that was because he never mentioned his land. To anyone, because it was private. It was his. He sent so much of his money home, to his mother and his sisters, but he'd also always put some aside for him. Because he had no intention of going out the way so many of the other riders seemed to. Spiraling down when their glory days were done, into this or that abyss, debt or gambling or the bottle. Hell no. The minute Cody had found this particular parcel of land, he'd known he was looking at his future. He'd put down the money years ago. Because he didn't think he'd be much help to anyone else if he couldn't help himself first, and the way things went with his family, it was a good bet they'd need some help down the road. And if not them, the many bull riders he'd known over the years who, like him, didn't have much to go home to when they weren't on tour.

Cody had never told another living soul about it, until now.

"It's in Northern California," he said gruffly. "I don't mean anywhere near San Francisco. There's a whole lot of

California above the Bay Area, which no one ever seems to talk about. And that's a good thing because it means they stay away."

"The only thing I really know about California," Skylar said after a moment, that same wariness making her gaze seem more than simply blue, somehow, "is that my sister lives there. She's never mentioned her position on what's actually considered Northern California, though. But maybe that's because she lives in San Francisco."

"I want to show it to you," Cody told her. He took the bag of frozen berries off his knee and put it on the table beside him as if it was a task that required his full, intense concentration. "My land, not San Francisco. I think you'll like it."

That sat there between them for a minute. And he knew—he could see—that Skylar knew perfectly well that it was about more than a plot of land that he wanted to show her. Maybe she could even see how little he wanted this to end, how frustrating he found the fact she gave herself to him without giving him *her,* and all the rest of the shit he had no intention of saying out loud.

If she did, she kept it to herself. He watched a thousand emotions come and go in those fathomless blue eyes of hers, the only blue he'd ever seen to rival the Montana sky.

But when Skylar spoke again, her voice was soft. Sweet, with that morning scratchiness beneath it.

"I'd love to see it, Cody," she said.

And maybe he knew then that they were on borrowed time. Maybe it was the way she said his name, as if it was goodbye.

But there was a two-week break between shows and he had nowhere else to be. That meant he could take his time driving them down from Tacoma to his pretty little bit of land on the moody Northern California coast. They drove down to Olympia, then headed west to follow route 101 south, past Willapa Bay and then across the mouth of the great Columbia River to pretty little Astoria before heading out to the Pacific. Even in July, the coast of Oregon was cool and foggy. Rocky and atmospheric.

And when they crossed into California there were redwoods and the same rocky shoreline, and it was only an hour or so south of the border that his land stretched across a high bluff overlooking the ocean.

"How much land do you have?" Skylar asked on their first morning there. Cody had parked the Airstream high on the bluffs, where the Pacific Ocean brooded down below, and there were views in all directions.

He liked the views. But even more, he liked the expanse of all the land, his to do with as he wished. He liked that he owned something in this world and that it was his despite the vagaries of a bull's temperament or his own physical limitations.

"A lot, I guess," he said.

They were sitting outside, enjoying the foggy morning

with the promise of a hot day ahead once the sun rose high enough to burn the day blue. Skylar had made that coffee of hers that Cody was entirely too afraid was becoming an addiction.

Or maybe it wasn't the coffee that he was afraid he was addicted to.

"How cagey." She grinned at him, that crooked smile of hers that made him hurt in ways he liked less with every passing day, especially when she was wrapped up in jeans and a pair of his heavy socks and a blanket she was wearing as a coat. She should have looked like a homeless person and he should have been about as fascinated. But he thought it was possible she was even prettier than the Pacific Ocean showing off down below. "You know that's only going to make me more intrigued."

"I'm not being cagey." He scowled at the water because it was better than aiming it at her the way he wanted to do, and he knew it had nothing to do with the land. "I started with fifty acres. But every time more property goes up for sale around here, I buy it if I can. I don't actually know how much there is now. I only know that when I'm ready, I can build a house and have no neighbors in any direction. For miles."

"You really don't like neighbors. Or people of any kind, really."

He liked her. But he didn't say that. Cody tilted his head at the Airstream.

"The fact I'd rather drive myself from bull-riding event to bull-riding event all season and never stay in a hotel unless we're in a big-ass city where there's no place to park should maybe have clued you in."

But Skylar clearly knew he was spoiling for a fight. Because she only smiled at him as if he was being cute, then put her coffee down. She stood, dropping that blanket and stretching a little so her T-shirt rode up and showed him a swathe of her skin, and then she crawled into his lap.

Whether he wanted her to or not, he thought grumpily, but the truth was, he always wanted her to.

He always wanted her.

"Something wrong with your chair?" he muttered, but her mouth was already too close to his.

"I think it broke," she said, and kissed him.

And he let her. Because of course he let her. But Cody knew within days that he'd made a mistake.

Because all Skylar wanted was a fling and he'd brought her here, to his land, the only thing he had that was entirely his. The only thing he had that was permanent.

And he had absolutely no trouble whatsoever seeing her here. With him. Forever.

Maybe he'd known he wanted to see if he'd feel that way when he brought her down here. When he could have let her leave him in Tacoma and he probably should have. He could have dropped her off at the airport and gone his merry way. He could have been sitting right here enjoying his solitude and the view.

But instead there was Skylar humming to herself as she cooked dinner, or dancing around while he did it. Instead there were the stories she told him about growing up in Billings years ago, well in advance of the hipster wave that had found the place these days.

"Who wants coffee in a *mason jar*?" she demanded, filled with outrage Cody didn't think was feigned. "Aside from being obnoxious on about seven different levels, a to-go latte in a mason jar is just awkward."

"Did it taste good?" he asked.

"That's not the point."

His trouble was, he liked her stories. He liked making her laugh. He liked looking up from studying bull-riding videos of his heroes on YouTube to find her reading something on her e-reader with that fierce concentration on her face and her fingers tugging on her bottom lip.

It would have been one thing if all he liked about her was the sex. It would have made everything much easier.

And maybe he'd been kidding himself all this time. Maybe he was getting a little bit too lost in the fantasy of the house he'd build here, where every window looked out on forever and there was no violence, no stepfathers, no shouting and drunkenness. Maybe this wasn't going to be the safe place for Kasey and Kathleen that he'd imagined it would be. Maybe he was getting carried away imagining a woman living here, lighting up the place, who looked a lot like

Skylar.

Because she didn't want him. Not the way he was more surprised every day to discover he wanted her. The way he'd never wanted anyone else, ever.

And if he had any doubt about that, if he'd somehow convinced himself that she just played her cards close to her chest and possibly felt all the same unwieldy and raw things he did, she disabused him of that notion the morning she looked up from her laptop when he shuffled into the Airstream's bright and sunny kitchen, aimed her crooked smile at him, and told him she needed a ride to the nearest airport.

"Which I'm pretty sure is in Eureka," she said in her calmest, most pleasant voice, as if she was moments away from spontaneous laughter. He wanted to put holes in his walls. "At least as best as I can tell from the map. Anyway, I hope it is, because I'm flying out of there. Today."

Chapter Eleven

"WHAT ARE YOU talking about?"

Cody didn't sound like himself.

But then, he hadn't really been himself since that day in Billings when he'd wandered around a party looking for Skylar instead of leaving the minute he could. And more than that, he was an idiot, because he should have known this was coming. How many times had she told him that she was going to leave? How many times had she packed her stuff?

The fact he wanted her to stay didn't mean she wanted it too.

Her smile didn't tumble off her face at the admittedly belligerent sound of his voice, but he thought it trembled a little bit. Still, that blue gaze of hers was clear as it met his.

"My brother is still getting married this weekend," she said softly. "That hasn't changed no matter what city we're in. Or what state. And this has been fun—"

"Don't."

He didn't exactly growl that, but it was close.

The only thing he could think was that he really should

have known that this was coming. Today. Because last night things had gotten intense. More intense than usual, that was. She'd clung to him, her mouth against his throat as she'd ridden him, her fingers digging into him so hard that she'd left marks.

He'd just been admiring those marks in his mirror.

He should have known.

Cody saw that he'd balled his hands into fists, right there where she could see it and possibly jump to all the wrong—or right—conclusions, and flattened out his hands.

Skylar shifted in her seat. She took a long time to close her laptop, staring at it fiercely as she did, and then another little while to lift her gaze to his again.

"I told you that I wasn't going to get the wrong idea," Skylar said, her voice even. Too even. Precise, like bullets.

Everything in Cody rebelled at that, and his temper skyrocketed. And he couldn't remember the last time he'd lost his temper. Not really. He spent a lot of time pretty grumpy, sure, but he never actually lost his grip. It had been years since he'd worried he might not be able to control himself, and before now it had always had something to do with Meredith and her life choices—like Todd.

But right now there was no family member in sight and he wanted nothing more than to yell his head off. Make enough noise to rock the trailer and better yet, get Skylar's attention. But he didn't.

He didn't yell. He didn't keep his hands in fists. He

didn't move further down the trailer's little walk space and put his hands on her, the way he wanted to do.

The way everything in him demanded that he do, right now.

"I told you from the start that I wasn't going to ask you for more than you can give," Skylar told him in that same *precise* voice. He hated it. "Not then, not now. Not ever. I meant it."

"Maybe you should." Cody's voice was tight. Dark. A little too close to mean. "Maybe you should ask for something, Skylar. Anything."

She lifted her chin like that was a hit. "That's not what this is."

"What's fucked up," he said, not sure he was controlling anything about his voice at all and not sure he cared anymore, "is that you don't seem to understand anything at all about what this is. You've refused to even consider it from the start."

"I know exactly what this is."

"No, darlin', you don't."

He raked his hands through his hair because he had too much temper slamming through him and it was the least aggressive thing he could think to do with them. And he shifted back, away from her, when what he wanted to do was go in the opposite direction. Get his hands on her, remind her of a few home truths—but he couldn't do that. Not now. Not with her looking at him like he was the one who'd gotten all this wrong.

"None of this is real for you," he gritted out. "You're on vacation. Maybe you think you're slumming, I don't know. But I do know that you're running away from something—"

"Don't be ridiculous."

"—or you'd answer your phone. It rings all the time. And the last time I saw you take a call was in Montana. I wanted to pretend you were just caught up with me, but we both know that's not true, don't we?"

She stood up then, in a rush. She slammed her hands on the table as she rose, as if she was thinking about using them on him. He wished she'd try.

"I'm not running away from anything and you spend a lot of time training and performing, Cody. You have no idea who I talk to when you're not around."

"Great. So you're hiding the fact you're with me. Even better."

"You're the one who's famous for this kind of thing," she threw at him. "Not me. Forgive me for not knowing the protocol."

"Here's a newsflash, Skylar. I'm famous for one great night, if you're lucky. Not this." He opened up his hands, taking in the whole of the Airstream. The land outside, stretching out for miles. The ocean down at the foot of the bluff. "This is my home. You think I bring anyone here? Because I don't. Only you."

"I didn't ask you to treat me any different."

"You don't ask for anything." And Cody could hear that his voice was too loud. But he didn't know how he could change that when he was holding on to his control by such a slim margin as it was. So he barreled on ahead. "And it's not because you don't want it. It's because you think you don't deserve it. Or whatever crazy thing you're telling yourself while your phone rings night and day, while you get so many texts you stopped checking them a week ago, and everyone you know is freaking out over the fact you came away with me. That tells me that none of this is what you do, Skylar. I knew that going in. So why don't you tell me why you're here?"

"I'm leaving," she said, and it sounded like the words were hard for her. As if she was biting back a storm and trying to sound calm while she did it. Or maybe Cody just wanted to believe that. "What does it matter what I was doing here?"

"I've spent all this time trying to figure out what makes a girl like you run away from everything she knows for some guy she met one night." Cody shook his head. "Some cowboy. But I can't figure it out. You think I can't tell that this isn't the kind of thing you do? You think I can't see that you're hiding things? You have ghosts in your eyes, Skylar. Sometimes they're all I can see."

She jerked at that, as if he'd thrown hot water on her. As if it burned.

"Are you my boyfriend, Cody?" she demanded, her blue

gaze dark and raw. "Do we share our emotions with each other—or anything else? Because I was under the impression that what we do is have sex. That's it."

"Because that's all you want." He threw the words at her like a punch, fast and brutal. "It's all you'll allow."

"My fiancé was killed."

It was like a sucker punch. It hit him hard, low in the gut; it took him a moment to find his breath again.

But she wasn't waiting for him to process what she'd said.

"Two years ago." Her voice was tight. Something too raw to be pure fury, but dark enough to match.

And he understood, then. The ghosts in her eyes, maybe, but also that she'd had no intention of ever telling him this. He'd brought her to his land and showed her what he held close, but she'd had no intention of letting him near hers.

Skylar was still talking in that same raw way. "He went out one night with friends. It was a Tuesday and an old friend was in town for business, so he went to meet him. He wasn't much for partying on the weeknights because he worked in finance and he liked his job, so he didn't expect it to be any kind of big night. It was just a random Tuesday."

And part of Cody wanted to stop her. Tell her she didn't have to tell him this, or anything.

But the truth was, he wanted to know. So he said nothing.

"I saw him before he left." Skylar didn't look particularly

emotional, or wrecked in any way, but he couldn't tell if that was a good thing or very, very bad. "I was an event planner and I'd spent all day mired in a huge corporate thing we were doing, so I was frazzled and cranky when I got home from work. He was getting ready to go out and I was still checking email, wishing that he and I could go out to a nice dinner. I was annoyed that he was going out with his friend—who I'd met in the past and didn't like that much—instead of doing something with me because I was in a mood. Not mad. Just a little annoyed."

Her smile seemed even more crooked than usual. "He kissed me goodbye the way he always did, he told me to take a bath and maybe rethink my attitude, and then he went out." She cleared her throat, as if it hurt. Or as if she'd laughed a little, then thought better of it. "And you know, I had a lovely little night. I poured myself a glass of wine, I took a long bath, and then I fell asleep on the couch watching old episodes of *Gilmore Girls*. And then there were police at my door."

She shrugged then, and that hurt. But Cody thought it hurt him more than her, if that was possible.

"And that was it," Skylar said. "I had one life when I fell asleep that night and another when I woke up. A drunk driver took him out while he was driving home. He had dinner and a couple of drinks, but his blood alcohol was well below the legal limit. Because that was who he was. Safe. Responsible. Good and kind. And some drunk idiot ran a red light, hopped a divider, and took him."

Cody kept his gaze on her as if the world would crumble into pieces if he looked away. He wanted to go to her, an impulse that he didn't entirely understand. He wanted to get his hands on her, as if to prove that she was still the woman he knew. Or maybe to remind her that she was. He wanted to pick her up, hold her in his arms, and chase the last of that darkness away from her face.

But he didn't do it.

Because maybe he was a bigger dick than he'd ever given himself credit for. Or maybe he knew, somehow, sympathy wasn't what she needed. Not from him. Not now, while she was busy using her ghosts as a weapon.

"So…what?" He made his voice bland to the point of insult, and knew he'd done the right thing in following that dark impulse when her gaze flashed bright again. It was better than that dull haze. It was better than ghosts. "Did you die too? Is that what this is about?"

"Thank you," Skylar said, and then she laughed, and Cody didn't know which one of them was more startled at the sound. "You're the first person in two years who's learned the tragic news about me and hasn't apologized. You're not sorry for my loss. You don't think that everything happens for a reason. I'm betting you're not about to tell me that when God closes a window he opens a door, or whatever. And honestly, that kind of makes me want to hug you."

Cody refused to let himself be distracted. "That's not

really answering the question."

Skylar took in a breath, then blew it out. Loud.

"I don't know," she told him, keeping up her chin. Maybe raising it a little, like she was contemplating taking a swing at him. "Maybe all the good parts of me died with him. Maybe that was it, my one good possible life, and it's gone. I don't have an answer to that."

"So this is what you do?" he asked, because he couldn't seem to stop himself. "You run around, fling after fling until you can't tell us apart, getting real good at temporary? Is that what you want?"

She blinked at him. "I'm sorry, did you actually ask me that? You?"

Cody was aware of the irony. It even stung a little. "I know what I'm talking about. That doesn't make me a hypocrite."

Or at least he didn't think it did.

And she looked too furious to call him on it. "This might come as a surprise, asshole, but you're it. You're my single fling. I'm pretty sure they call this the shameful, embarrassing rebound."

Cody shook his head at her. "Nice try, Skylar. But you're not ashamed or embarrassed. Do you think I can't tell? And don't kid yourself. I'm no rebound."

Something moved in her then, he could see it. For a moment she looked fragile, and his heart kicked at him. He wanted to put her back together if she broke. He wanted to gather up all those jagged little pieces and make her whole again. He didn't care if she was a little cracked, because he knew scars were beautiful. She'd showed him that.

But she recovered herself. That fragile expression disappeared, replaced by something fierce, and she didn't quite meet his gaze.

"I just need to get to the airport," she said quietly. "The novelty of you failing to express the slightest bit of sympathy is wearing off pretty quickly, it turns out."

"You think you're the only person in this world with pain?" he asked. "Because you're not."

"Yes," she bit out, and she was definitely looking at him then. Straight on, like she wanted to rip him into pieces. "I'm sure that you suffer terribly as you make your money, handle your fame, and navigate the attentions of all your buckle bunnies. I'm sure that's very difficult. My heart bleeds."

"My mother has always been a bitter woman," Cody told her, because he told this woman everything, apparently. He shared all the things he kept hidden, one after the next. "But when my father was alive, she was softer. She smiled more. Or at all. Now she smokes cigarettes and lets her new husband smack her around, because I think she thinks she deserves it." He let out a little bark of something that no one would describe as laughter. "Because she wasn't with him when some methed-out fool stole a car and rammed it through a busy intersection, taking out a mother with twin babies, two high school kids, and my father in one big, multi-car crash. So believe me, Skylar, I not only understand your pain, I've seen exactly what happens if you give in to it. I know what happens if you let it eat you whole."

"Are you talking about your mother? Or are you talking about you?"

"I'm not the one who packed up shop and called it done because somebody died," Cody said. Or maybe shouted. "I watched my mother do it and apparently, you're doing it too. Meanwhile, some of us dedicate our lives to taking care of what's left. I have two half-sisters. It's up to me to make sure that they are as protected from the things my mother can't control as possible. I pay for them. I keep them safe. I can't bring my father back, but I'll be damned if I'll die along with him."

"Well, aren't you the very image of an early Christian martyr?" Skylar seethed right back at him, even taking a step toward him as if she wanted nothing more than to swing at him. "How wonderful that you were able to take your own suffering and turn it into such a positive experience for everyone around you. I'm sure that's why you're known as the least approachable, most obnoxious member of the entire American Extreme Bull Riders Tour. I'm sure that's why not one person in the family and friends section had anything good to say about you that didn't relate to your skills on the back of a bull."

"Good. I take that as a compliment. I'm not there to

make friends."

"That's what sociopathic reality stars say," she hurled at him, taking another step toward him as if she couldn't help herself. "It's what people with absolutely no social skills and no grasp of reality say to cover the fact that they don't know how to forge relationships with anyone. In life, you make friends. You go out into the world and share experiences, and you do that *with people*."

She was breathing harder then, and her gaze was so bright it should have hurt. Him or her. Both of them.

And she was still talking. "People need people, Cody. That's what people are *for*. The fact that you're a veteran of the tour and have absolutely no friends says a great deal about you. None of it good."

"I appreciate the lecture," he drawled. "Especially from someone who's so great at forging relationships herself."

"I don't have any trouble with relationships."

"Yeah? When's the last time you answered a text? Or a phone call?"

"When's the last time anyone bothered to call you at all?" she retorted.

"You're so determined that this is a fling. Well guess what, Skylar? It's not. It never was. I set eyes on you standing there in your father's doorway and that was it."

Cody shouldn't have said that. He knew it was a mistake even as the words came out of his mouth, and not only because she took a step back as if he'd reached out and put his hands on her the way he wanted.

But that didn't make it any less true.

"The only reason you're even considering saying these things to me is because I told you I wasn't available." She let out a sound that he couldn't define. It lodged itself between his ribs, as if she'd broken one off and stabbed him with the jagged edge. "You think I don't know how men operate? Especially men like you?"

"You sure seem to know a whole hell of a lot about men like me. When I'm pretty sure you've never met one before."

"You're a bull rider," she said, and her voice was scratchy, but not from sleep this time. And she made his profession, his calling and his love, sound like his doom. "You spend your entire life chasing eight seconds. You want things you can't keep. And you don't want me. Not really." She raised her hands, then dropped them back to her sides. "You don't even know me."

"And whose fault is that?" Cody demanded.

Skylar didn't say anything for a long moment. Then another. She stared down at the floor instead, and Cody was sure he could feel her temper. Or maybe that was his, making his heart pound too hard. Making every muscle in his body clench tight.

Making him want nothing more than to do all of this over. To do something—anything—that would keep her from going down this path in the first place. Or to keep his own big mouth shut instead of making everything worse.

"I don't want to do this." Her voice was quiet when she spoke again, but intense. "I'm not going to do this."

And Cody stood there. Because he didn't dare move. He stood where he was as she gathered her things from the table, then walked toward the back of the trailer, skirting around him without so much as brushing against him. It took some doing. And it infuriated him. But he knew that if he did anything—if he so much as breathed on her—he would sweep her up into his arms and try to reach her a little more directly, and he was pretty sure that she'd hate him for that.

If she wanted to know the truth about them, she wouldn't be leaving him. Not like this.

He stood there, staring at nothing, and tried to wrestle himself under control.

He could hear her back in the bedroom, and he knew what she was doing. Packing that same damn bag that she'd already packed a couple of times now. Maybe she'd never really unpacked it. He should have known from the start how this was going to go. He should have understood what he was getting into.

Maybe if he had, he would have kept a few of his own secrets in reserve.

He heard her come out of the bedroom behind him, and then pause.

"I'm going to call a car," she said, and she was using that voice again. He remembered it from all those weeks ago in Billings. So calm. So even.

So full of shit.

But he didn't call her on it. Because wasn't that the point she been trying to make? It wasn't his place to call her on anything.

"I'll take you," he told her.

"It would probably be better if you didn't. All things considered."

"I might not be the man you want," Cody said in as even a voice as he could rustle up on short notice, "but I'm a man, Skylar. And a man doesn't leave a woman out in the middle of nowhere to find her own way home, no matter how many unfortunate words got thrown around one morning in a trailer. I'll take you." But he said it calmly. Almost easily. "And I don't know where you think you are, but there are no cars to call out here."

He heard the way she let out a breath behind him.

And he knew how to do this. He knew the dance. The rawness of it, the wild magic, good or bad. How to lean into the jolts and ride out the bumps, making it all look like grace.

He knew what to do when it was over. How to disengage and roll until he was free.

Cody had managed to get off the backs of more bulls than he could count. Hundreds and hundreds of qualified rides, and that didn't even count all the times he hadn't made it to the full eight seconds. And he'd gotten off every one of them, one way or another.

Pretty or ugly, he usually managed it without breaking every bone in his body—even if sometimes, he came away battered and limping and in need of a little medical attention.

He could do this, too.

So he turned around, he made himself smile, and then Cody set about letting her go.

Chapter Twelve

THE TOWN OF Marietta, nestled at the mouth of Paradise Valley east of Bozeman, was possibly Skylar's favorite place in the whole, wide world, and she was determined to be happy she was back.

Because she was always happy when she was in Marietta. That was what Marietta was *for,* she'd always thought, on all those trips they'd taken from Billings over the years and all the extended family holidays since.

Her ancestors had come here hundreds of years ago, out into the untamed wilds of Montana where there were rumors of copper in the hills and railway barons were laying claim to wide swathes of the glorious western landscape. And more to the point, far away from the reach of Boston authorities. Skylar felt that same pull every time she found herself in the sturdy, pretty little western town at the foot of Copper Mountain where Greys had lived since before there was a Marietta or really anything but hardy prospectors with more inbred, bone-deep stubbornness than sense.

Her uncle Jason ran the saloon that had been a mainstay of the area since the pre-Marietta days, and Skylar thought that if she squinted she could see old-time cowboys swaggering down Main Street with itchy trigger fingers while fancy ladies plied their trade from the upstairs balcony of Grey's the way they had back when.

The summer evening was that impossible dark blue edging into full black as she walked down the street with her sister and Scottie's absurdly attractive boyfriend, Damon. Marietta was filled to bursting with Greys this weekend, which was just the way Skylar liked it best. Her grandparents had moved out to Big Sky a while back, a valley or two over, but were staying in Marietta to be closer to all the wedding festivities—like tonight's rehearsal dinner that Jesse and Michaela had thrown at the recently restored Crawford House Museum way up at the top of Black Bart Road.

Skylar had stood on the lawn of gorgeous old *grande dame* of a house she'd always wanted to peek into when she was a kid, looking down over the stretch of mountains in the distance and Marietta down there on either side of the river, and she'd felt something in her battered, half-frozen heart swell.

As if maybe she wasn't as battered or frozen as she imagined.

And more, as if this was a homecoming, this weekend with her family in a place she would always think of as theirs no matter who else might live in it. This celebration of love and laughter and two people finding each other against all odds that made her long for all the things she knew she couldn't have.

But the man she thought of when her stomach knotted up wasn't the one she'd lost. It was the one she'd left.

Skylar didn't want to think about Cody.

Not tonight. Not when she was surrounded by so many members of her family, all of whom had entirely too many opinions about how she'd spent the last few weeks of her life. She'd been contending with them since she'd arrived late the night before. All those miles, all those states she'd flown over, all that distance between her and Cody now, and she still felt him as if he was right beside her.

As if he'd wormed his way deep into her heart, and was now in residence there, when she'd been so certain that could never happen.

You will never be free of him, a small voice inside her had intoned while she'd stood on the edge of the sweeping Crawford House lawn. *It's like he marked you.*

And the crazy part was, something in her had thrilled a little to that idea.

"Did you see Grandma's face?" Scottie was asking the whole of Main Street, laughing into the gathering night as they walked from Damon's rented SUV toward Grey's, where the rehearsal dinner after party was taking place. "I've always heard the expression 'she looked like she was sucking on a lemon,' but I don't think I've ever actually seen lemon-sucking face in action before. Until tonight."

"It was a lot of lemon," Damon agreed in that low, lazy

way of his.

Damon was problematic. He was as shockingly good-looking as Skylar remembered—though she and her cousin Luce had been forced to confess that they'd actually down-graded him in their minds because who could be that attractive? All that dark black hair and bright blue eyes. He had *big-city rich guy* written all over him, which would have made a lesser man look silly on a Montana street. But not Damon. He looked like there wasn't a place in all the world where he wouldn't feel perfectly at his ease.

And Scottie herself looked as happy as Skylar had ever seen her. Certainly much happier than she had throughout her pointless Alexander years, the ex no one missed, least of all Scottie. She and Damon were never not touching each other. They weren't all over each other like teenagers in the back of a movie theater, like some couples Skylar could name—her loved-up and hugely pregnant cousin Christina, for example, who hung on her longtime and clearly equally besotted husband Dare as if they'd just met and didn't already have a toddler—but still. They were always in contact.

It made Skylar's chest feel a little tight.

"Grandma's face is a work of angry art," Skylar agreed. "I don't think she's liked a single thing in the last thirty years."

Elly Grey was a Marietta institution. She was famous for her bad temper, her husband's wandering eye, her boundless disappointment in three of her four adult children, and the trickle-down dismay she felt for all of her grandchildren. Even the occasion of Jesse's wedding couldn't make her feel any better about the whole lot of them. She'd sat at her place at the table, shooting irritated looks at Grandpa as he'd enjoyed himself a drink, and pursing up her lips every time Billy or Uncle Jason or dizzy Aunt Melody opened their mouths. It was only Christina and Luce's father Ryan that she liked, something she made absolutely clear whenever possible, because he'd married Aunt Gracie right out of high school and they'd been together ever since.

"What I love is that it's all seemed to turn a corner lately," Scottie said now. "Maybe the famous Grey Curse is a thing of the past."

You're all cursed, Grandma had said one Thanksgiving a few years back to her own flesh and blood, because that was how she liked to celebrate. *Blood will tell.*

Skylar smiled as wide as she could as they walked up to the old, western-style doors of Grey's Saloon. Damon held the door for them, and Scottie grabbed Skylar's arm as they walked inside as if they were walking into a theme park. Because in a way, they were. The Grey Family Adventure.

The saloon was exactly as it always was, deceptively simple and rustic, with Uncle Jason already back behind the bar and his saloon manager, a-Grey-in-all-but-name Reese Kendrick at his side. And a couple of Uncle Jason's usually absent daughters there besides, Rayanne and Joey, helping their father sling drinks to a crowd that was almost entirely relatives or other wedding guests.

Some things never changed. Grey's was one of them. The Grey Curse was another. When Grandma had issued her dire proclamation, most of the cousins had been about as unlucky in love as it was possible to get. Most of their parents redefined unhappiness, so it made sense they'd follow suit. Uncle Jason was surly and gruff and never spoke about the wife who'd just up and left him and their girls one day. Aunt Melody flitted from one bad decision to the next, though at least she'd had the sense to stop having babies after she'd had Devyn and Sydney with different fathers. The same, of course, could not be said for Billy.

It had seemed for a long time that the cousins were destined to follow suit. The oldest Grey cousin, Lorelai, had all but fallen off the face of the planet—probably because she had a complicated history with Reese and a fractious relationship with her father, Jason. Her sisters Rayanne and Joey weren't any luckier in love, though at least they bothered to come home every now and again. Jesse had sworn off women after Angelique and Billy had gotten together, at least for more than a night or two. Scottie had lived with Alexander for years while he'd cheated on her. Luce had kicked out her high school sweetheart Hal after she finally got sick enough of his cheating.

None of you know a single thing about longevity, Grandma had thundered, forever more Calamity Jane than Mrs. Butterworth, because she was nothing like other people's soft, sweet, pancake-flipping grandmothers.

But things were changing. Christina and Dare had been on the verge of divorce, but had worked it out to the tune of giddiness and babies. Jesse was so happy with Michaela that he was actually getting married in a big ceremony to celebrate it, involving the entire family and most of Montana, it seemed. Even Scottie, having dated that idiot all through college and law school and well into her life in San Francisco, had finally found Damon. For a long time, Skylar had considered herself evidence that the curse wasn't a thing. That it was just something Grandma had said because she liked to say mean things, because she was one of those old women with a sharp tongue and no boundaries.

Of course, after she'd lost Thayer, Skylar had been pretty sure that she was Exhibit Number One that the curse lived on.

Now she didn't know what the hell she was.

"I have absolutely no doubt that every last one of us will live happily ever after," Skylar assured her sister as they moved further into the throng. Because if the possessive look in Damon's eyes every time he looked at Scottie was any guide, that was certainly going to be true for them.

Skylar was a little less sure about herself.

But the great thing about a huge family wedding was that it allowed Skylar to wander around Grey's as if she was a local. As if she knew everybody—because tonight, as a sister of the groom, she kind of did. There were locals that she had never met before, like local microbrewery-owner Jasper Flint of FlintWorks and his schoolteacher wife Chelsea, who entertained Skylar with stories of Copper Mountain Rodeo shenanigans a few years running. Or local tattoo artist Griffin Hyatt and his wife Emmy, who confided in Skylar that Jesse and Michaela had gotten matching tattoos as an engagement gift to themselves.

"If they're not sharing their tattoos, Bug, we probably shouldn't either," Griffin said mildly after Emmy tried to draw a picture of the outline of Grey's Saloon that Jesse and Michaela supposedly now both had stamped on their bodies in the air before her.

Emmy, who neither looked like a bug nor appeared to mind being called one, wrinkled up her nose at her husband, who had visible tattoos and the kind of still, watchful readiness that made any red-blooded woman look at him twice. Once because of that vibe he gave off that made him look like some kind of athlete. And again because he was silly hot, with all those tattoos besides.

"It's not like they got them in sensitive areas. How private can they be?"

"Isn't it the kiss of death to get matching tattoos?" Skylar asked, laughing. She saw Jesse and Michaela standing over near the bar with some of Michaela's local relatives, neither looking as if they were being stalked by the actual, known and proven curse of tattooing their love on each other. "Just look at any celebrity breakup. I thought the minute anyone got a tattoo about their relationship, much less matching ones, the relationship is pretty much instantly doomed."

"That's only if you use actual names," Griffin assured her, his eyes gleaming. "There's something about putting a name on skin that ruins everything. No name, no problem."

"We don't have commemorative tattoos, if you're wondering," Emmy said then. "Because I'm with you. That's crazy."

And then they were drawn into a conversation with other locals about the possibility that the Copper Mountain Rodeo wouldn't happen this year, and Skylar drifted away.

She talked to as many of her relatives as she could find, while giving her grandparents a wide berth. It wasn't exactly a hardship. Her cousins were an endless source of entertainment for her, because she loved nothing more than catching up with them and seeing what was going on in their always-interesting lives. For example, Luce, the cousin who'd stayed right here in Marietta, always made Skylar laugh. Because as far she could tell, Luce had been pissed off about pretty much everything since grade school.

"Is it delightful?" Christina asked when Skylar advanced that theory over a game of pool. "Or is she a rageaholic?"

"Don't let her hear you call her that," Dare muttered. "Or you'll experience it firsthand."

"I would never be so silly as to get on Luce's bad side," Skylar assured them with a laugh.

And then she went off to mingle some more, ignoring

that restless feeling in the pit of her stomach that made her feel like she was that character in a fairy tale, forced to keep dancing or she'd burst into flame.

It had been all *rush rush rush* since she'd left California. Cody had dropped her off at the airport in Eureka—but she wasn't letting herself think about him, not here in public—and she'd been running around ever since. One airport to another. Then the car ride into Marietta. Then racing around today doing last-minute bridesmaid things and generally making herself available to Michaela as needed.

Anything and everything to block the past three weeks from her mind.

It's absolutely working, she told herself staunchly. *You're totally fine.*

But she launched herself at a table of Michaela's Seattle friends—including noted famous computer genius Amos Burke, who was surprisingly friendly for a man who encouraged people to think of him as an eccentric hermit—just to make sure she couldn't take a breath and question that.

"I'm glad you decided to come," Angelique said stiffly, when Skylar couldn't avoid it any longer and found herself face-to-face with her stepmother.

She clenched her bottle of local beer, called Triple C, and wished she could chug it twice. "I was always coming to Jesse's wedding, Angelique."

Her stepmother lifted one shoulder, then dropped it. "I don't know how anyone would know whether you were or not. You fell off the face of the planet for weeks."

"It was three weeks. I think some people spend longer than that on a shopping trip."

"You could have let us know you were okay," Angelique said, her voice as brittle as the way she held herself. "Or answered a call. I don't think it would have killed you."

And so many things bubbled up inside Skylar then. The injustice of all this, of course. The urge to smack Angelique down, put her in her place, remind her that she was in no position to judge anyone—particularly not a stepdaughter who was the same age as she was. To say nothing of Angelique's own dirty little past with Billy.

But this was a wedding, not a bruising family dinner in her grandma's inimitable style. And if Jesse could see his way clear to spending time with Angelique and Billy without losing his cool, Skylar had no excuse not to do the same.

She took a deep breath, then let it go. She made herself count to ten.

"I don't understand what this is," she said quietly. When Angelique stiffened, she reached out and hooked her hand around her stepmother's bony wrist, to show she wasn't launching an attack. "You're acting as if I hurt your feelings. And I'm not trying to be rude, Angelique, but I don't understand how this has anything to do with you. Why are you so upset?"

Angelique looked as if she hadn't expected the question. And something in her face changed, then. That brittleness disappeared and she blinked, as if she was considering what Skylar had said.

"I guess I thought that everything would go differently," she said after a minute.

"So did I," Skylar said dryly.

"That's not what I mean," Angelique replied. "When you moved back to Billings, I thought it would be a good thing for you. For me. For your dad and Lacey and Layla. All of us."

Skylar squeezed her wrist, then let go. "Of course it was a good thing. You gave me somewhere to go after Atlanta and I appreciate that more than you know."

Angelique's lovely face shifted into something wry, reminding Skylar that when she'd first met her, years back at that fateful Christmas when she'd been Jesse's girlfriend, Skylar had imagined they'd be friends. Good friends, even. It made her heart thud a little too hard to remember that now.

Maybe, that voice inside of her that seemed to get more strident by the minute said loudly, *you should think about practicing a little forgiveness. Inside and out.*

Angelique shrugged, and she didn't look like a wounded stepmother, or the model she'd been, or Jesse's big mistake. She just looked like a woman with a complicated past and a possibly messy life, like anyone else.

Like Skylar.

"I guess I thought that it was my chance to prove that I wasn't the monster that everybody thinks I am," Angelique said simply. "I thought if I could take care of you, I could actually do something for this family. Instead of being Billy's little embarrassment." She smiled slightly, though it didn't quite reach her eyes. "I guess that was stupid."

And Skylar didn't have it in her to lash out at that. To parse every word and look for signs of self-pity and judge her stepmother's right to say something like that.

It would have been different three weeks ago, she understood in a sudden flash. Before she'd followed her heart, and maybe other parts, into something that absolutely nobody understood. It would have been different if she had still been the grieving almost-widow she'd been when she arrived in Montana. But she wasn't that Skylar anymore. Maybe that was the trouble. She still didn't know who the hell she was.

And yet she found that there was space inside of her for compassion, when she would have said her stepmother didn't deserve any. But she knew what it felt like now. She knew what it was like to stand in this great big mess of Greys and know that everyone in the room was talking about her business. She knew what it was like to be the subject of whispers, weird texts, and too much speculation.

"You don't have to prove anything, Angelique," she said, very distinctly. "The only person whose opinion you need to worry about is my father's. He's the one you married." She lifted her beer bottle and tilted it, like some kind of salute. Or a toast to fallen women, maybe, like the ones who had lived and worked in these walls so long ago. "All these people are going to talk about you no matter what you do. You might as well do what makes you happy."

"Are you happy?" Angelique asked after a moment, an assessing sort of light in her gaze. "Are you really?"

And Skylar couldn't have said why that caught at her. Maybe it was because she thought Angelique really meant it. She was really asking. She wasn't trying to prove a point and she didn't appear to have an agenda. Unlike every other person who'd set up that same question like a trap for Skylar to stumble into, Angelique was actually asking as if she wanted to know the answer.

But Skylar didn't know it herself.

"That's a complicated question," she murmured, surprised to feel her throat a little tight with emotion. "I'm going to have to get back to you on that."

She moved away from Angelique when one of Michaela's relatives interrupted them, smiling as she went. She flitted from one knot of wedding guests to another, laughing with her family and avoiding more speculation by guiding the conversation away from her recent behavior. She was good at guiding. She watched Michaela, looking as pretty as any bride should in a bright blue dress that made her dark hair and hazel eyes seem to glow. Or then again, maybe that was the bright love that gleamed between Michaela and Jesse, evident even when they stood on different sides of the saloon.

Evident even to her and that battered, frozen heart of

hers that seemed less and less either one of those things with every passing moment.

"I thought you were bringing your new man," Jesse said when she found herself next to him, because he was always irritating. Even the night before his wedding.

"I would think you have a whole lot more to worry about than my love life," Skylar said mildly. "Like how tomorrow you're going to have Mom and Dad in the same room for the first time since the divorce. How's that going to happen? Without blood, I mean."

Jesse shot her a look that told her he wasn't the least bit fooled by the change in subject.

"Funny you should ask, because I've had to set that shit up like I'm personally storming the beaches of Normandy." He started counting off on his fingers. "Different entrances. Different tables. A major conversation with Dad about how no amount of drinks should lead him to believe that it's time to make nice with Mom because she hates him and thinks he's literally the devil. You know, the usual."

"He's going to do it anyway," Skylar said, with a little laugh, more because it was inevitable than funny. "You must know that. He's going to get all liquored up and roll right up to Mom and she's going to lose her mind. She's going to start flipping tables in the middle of your wedding reception."

"She better not touch the tables. You have no idea how much work went into those tables."

"Jesse. Please." Skylar realized that she was enjoying herself, and ran with it. She grinned at her brother. "Mom has been waiting years for the opportunity to play the victim in front of such a large audience. You need to expect the drama. It's the only way to contain it."

"Congratulations, Skylar. I'm recruiting you to make sure that nothing happens. I told Mom that if she came, she had to leave the voodoo dolls at home."

Skylar shrugged. Expansively. "I don't know what you think I can do to prevent the inevitable carnage. Mom and Dad are going to be Mom and Dad, no matter where they are. No matter what else is going on. No matter how much you beg them not to be, or appeal to their better angels, or threaten them. It's like you've blocked out our entire childhood."

"I just try to repress it," Jesse said. "Actively. But think about Michaela. And poor Damon. We can't let them see behind the curtain to the realities of the Grey Curse, or how will we ever break it? They'll run screaming." He grinned that grin of his that Skylar had long suspected ruined the lives of most of the poor Seattle women who'd been on the receiving end of it all these years. "Don't do it for me, Skylar. Do it for the cousins. Do it to break the curse and prove Grandma wrong."

"I also wouldn't want Michaela to realize that she really is too good for you," Skylar said thoughtfully, biting back her own grin. "She hasn't made any vows yet. She could still make a break for it."

"Don't think I don't know it," Jesse agreed, though he didn't seem particularly concerned. Then his gaze got entirely too knowing. "Back to the far more interesting topic of your rodeo situation, which believe me, is all anyone wants to talk about when you're not in the room."

"That's obviously just what I wanted to hear. Thank you."

"Naturally, I tell everyone to grow up and leave you alone, even in your absence, because that's the kind of excellent older brother I am." He did no such thing. Skylar didn't have to see that gleam in his eyes to know that full well. "So, adult to adult and not behind your back like everyone else, where's your man?"

"I had no idea you were this interested in my social life," Skylar said coolly, wishing she'd thought to get another drink or ten. "You never have been before."

"You've never had a social life before." Jesse snorted. "As far as I can tell this is the only time you've ever done anything with anyone."

He didn't say, except for Thayer. That part was implied.

"You don't actually know whether or not that's true," Skylar pointed out. "Maybe I'm just a little bit better about keeping my private life private than you are. Maybe I don't really want every single member of my extended family commenting on all my stuff all the time. *Maybe* I'm not an exhibitionist."

"Then you picked the wrong summer to play tempt me, cowboy, with a bull rider," Jesse said with a laugh. "For future reference, get your crazy on when there's not a family wedding in the middle of it all. It makes it much harder for everybody to compare notes."

"I'll keep that in mind."

"And if you like this guy, Skylar?" Jesse's gaze met hers unflinchingly then. "Then like him. What does it matter what anyone else thinks? You were not put on this earth to make anybody happy but you."

But his words hit her hard, right in the heart that wasn't nearly as frozen as it should have been. As it had been three weeks ago.

"I'm pretty sure it's that exact attitude that led Dad to every single terrible decision he's ever made," Skylar said, her voice a little rougher than planned.

"You need to stop comparing yourself to Dad, because you're nothing like him," Jesse said, with a tremendous confidence that Skylar wanted to cling to. That she wanted, more than anything, to share. "You don't have a wife. You don't have kids. You don't answer to anybody but yourself. Sure, your entire family is comprised of nosy, gossiping bastards, but you don't owe anybody anything, Skylar. You've been through enough. If this guy makes you happy, then Jesus Christ. *Be happy.*"

Skylar shook her head, blinking back the sudden onslaught of emotion she didn't know quite how to deal with.

"I don't know if I remember how."

Jesse slung an arm around her shoulder and held her tight for a moment.

"Then it's about time you figured it out," he said gruffly. "Don't you think?"

But she didn't get a chance to answer him, because he was swept up in an excited little scrum of his friends, all of them shouting out something that sounded like a chant. Skylar let him go. Because maybe she was reeling a little bit.

Or a lot.

She stood on the outskirts of the party, soaking it all in, trying to get her bearings again. There was something about these walls, she thought. Something about Grey's Saloon. The fact that it had stood just shy of forever right here on this very spot. She thought about all the stories the walls could tell, all the tales that had bled into the floorboards across the years. Prospectors and cowboys, loose women and rough miners. Railway barons and ranchers, stretching back generations. The history of Montana was soaked straight into the foundations, and she thought that if she curled her toes, she could channel a little bit of that fortitude herself.

Because this was Montana. This had been the frontier and in many ways still was. And people died out here all the time. Good deaths, bad deaths. Hangings and robberies, childbirth and murder. The entire world was a story of death, one way or another, and that was only as sad as she chose to make it.

Because life went on.

The Marietta settlers had forged their lives out here in the unforgiving terrain. They'd fought off predators, rustlers, outlaws, and most unforgiving of all, the endless Montana winters. They'd raised families and buried them, too. Some much, much earlier than planned.

And above all, they'd persevered.

Skylar had always admired the history here. She'd always loved that her family was so steeped in it.

But it had never really crossed her mind to think about how much history had to teach her.

Most of all, that everybody died, sooner or later. And she didn't want the rest of her life to be disfigured by Thayer's death. She didn't want to live in that kind of fear, that made every day she drew breath a half-life of survivor's guilt and *what ifs*. She didn't want to be that kind of zombie, shuffling through what was left of her time, never really living. Never hoping. Never challenging herself to move on.

Never letting her heart do what it did best. Beat. Skip. *Love.*

Cody was right. She'd been hiding herself in plain sight ever since Thayer had died. She'd been frozen so long that she couldn't even identify it herself. Cody had thawed her out. He'd reminded her what it was like to be alive, alight, filled with heat and fire and life and love instead of tears.

She didn't know if she had a future with him. But wasn't that the point of these last, hard years? No one ever knew.

Nothing was ever certain. You could make all the plans in the world and it wouldn't matter on a random, otherwise unremarkable Tuesday.

Skylar didn't know what was in store for her and Cody, if anything, but she didn't need to know.

What she did know was that she needed to stop lying to herself and to him. They both deserved better.

She'd walked away from him as if she never meant to return, and she'd seen the look on his face, both in the Airstream and when he'd dropped her off at the airport in all that simmering, painful silence. But that was the good thing about getting in over her head with a man who was booked into arenas every single weekend for the foreseeable future. It wasn't as if he could hide on the back of the bull.

She would get through this wedding. She would continue to smile and laugh and do everything in her power to convince her family that she was fine. Because she thought that after all this, the simple truth was that she really, truly was.

Perfectly fine. At last.

And maybe that was what she'd really been hiding from these last three weeks.

Because some part of her thought that if she was fine, she was betraying Thayer's memory. That her friends and his family down in Atlanta were right and she was supposed to be that shrine to him, forever.

Even if she'd outgrown it.

The door slammed open down at the other end of the saloon, and Skylar didn't know what made her look up at the sound. People had been coming and going all night, boisterous and happy and filled with the usual giddy wedding fever, in little groups of family and friends and guests.

But she knew in a single glance that the man who stood there—dressed like a cowboy, black hat, granite jaw, and a thousand-yard stare like a gunslinger of old—was different.

Mine, a little voice inside her whispered, as if it knew.

As if it had always known.

Because it was Cody.

Of course, at last, it was Cody.

And just in case Skylar still had the smallest doubt about the things she was afraid to feel for this man, they all boiled up in her then. She felt her heart slam at her. Her stomach knotted up and between her legs, she melted.

She was too hot. Too cold. Some kind of fever, and she'd felt it before. She knew it was him.

It had always been him.

She stayed where she was and waited for him to see her. It didn't take him more than a second or two. His hard gaze swept the room, taking in assorted Greys in the midst of their celebrations, and then finding her unerringly. As if he'd known where she was all along.

As if all of this was inevitable.

Marietta wasn't her home, not really. But it had always felt as if it should have been. And yet nothing felt more like home than the instant burst of heat and flame in Cody's gaze when it met hers. Or the way he started toward her, with that swagger that announced who and what he was in no uncertain terms, loud enough to be heard all over Marietta and up to the very peak of Copper Mountain high above it.

He was the kind of man who walked where he wanted and let the crowd rearrange themselves around him, and that was exactly what they did. It was as if they cleared a path. Skylar knew, on some level, that her cousins were picking up on the way this strange man locked on to her and stalked toward her. She was even more sure that most of them knew exactly who he was, and not only because these were Montana people and bull-riding fans.

But she couldn't seem to make herself care about any of that, because he was here. Cody was right here in Marietta when she'd left him early yesterday morning in California.

And it was time to put her money where her mouth was.

Chapter Thirteen

"WHAT ARE YOU doing here?" Skylar asked him when he finally drew close, because she couldn't think of what else to say.

But he clearly didn't like that. His dark green eyes glittered, and that jaw of his was set at a stubborn tilt. There was something about a man in a cowboy hat, especially when it wasn't a prop. She suddenly felt sorry for all those bulls he'd conquered over the years. They'd never had a chance.

"Nice to see you too, Skylar," he drawled, and it was the same as it always was. Fire and need, rushing through her and pooling there, low in her belly. "This is called a grand gesture."

She wasn't sure she could process this. She'd been thinking about him and now here he was. It was like magic. Or possibly it was the nervous breakdown everyone seemed to think she had coming. Maybe he wasn't here at all—but no. She saw her sister standing a ways behind him, and Scottie was grinning entirely too wide for Cody to be a hallucination.

Then she made it clear he was real by shooting Skylar a

thumbs-up.

"I didn't think you made grand gestures," she managed to say, returning her attention to the cowboy who was still simmering in front of her, all hard expression and that body made of steel and determination.

"I ride bulls," Cody growled. "My life is a grand gesture."

She conceded the point with a faint nod of her head.

"Let me break this down for you," he continued when she didn't speak. Because she couldn't. "About five seconds after you got out of my truck, I decided this was all bullshit. By the time I parked, you were through security—and, Skylar, you still haven't given me your goddamned phone number."

"I told you my number in Billings."

"It isn't in my phone."

Because they hadn't been apart. Because there had been no reason to call when she was always right there.

But she assumed he didn't care about any of that, if the way he was looking at her then was any guide. All dark and grim and somehow beautiful.

"You didn't tell me where you were going, so I had to figure it out," Cody said in the same pissed-off growl that probably shouldn't have made every part of her hum in a deep delight. "I put together all the pieces of the stories you told me about your family in Marietta and your brother in order to figure out where he might be getting married. I had to do a little detective work to make sure that I was right.

Then I had to drive all night and all day to get my ass to Montana from California. Don't ask me what I'm doing here. You know."

"Cody..."

Skylar didn't know where to start. She wanted to tell him about the history of Marietta and the history of her. She wanted to make him understand all the different contours of her heart, how it beat and what it needed, and how somehow, she felt safe for the first time in years when he was the one cradling it between his hands.

But she didn't know how to put that into words.

"Let's focus on the big picture," Cody said. He was moving again and it took Skylar a minute to realize that he was backing her up against the nearest wall. Because he didn't seem to care that the entirety of her family was watching him do this. He didn't appear to notice that there was anyone else in the room.

It was the hottest thing she'd ever seen.

Because he was giving her that focus of his, intense and intent. She'd seen that look on his face before. She saw it every time he dropped down onto the back of the bull. She saw it every time he lowered himself over her and thrust deep into her, as well.

She couldn't seem to help the shudder that overtook her at that.

"I'm in love with you," he told her gruffly. "And I get that you don't want to hear that. That doesn't change it.

Nothing's going to change it. I had some twenty hours of driving, over mountains, to talk myself out of it and it didn't take." He shook his head when she opened her mouth. "I know it's fast. It's straight-up crazy. But it is what it is. And you can take all the time in the world you need to get your head around it, I don't care."

Skylar cleared her throat, amazed he couldn't hear the way her pulse was kicking through her veins.

"That's very romantic," she managed to say after a moment. "It's amazing to me that some lucky woman hasn't already snapped you up."

"That's pretty funny, Skylar. Hilarious." His jaw seemed even harder. "That's what you do, isn't it? Deflect. Lie if you have to. But here's the thing: I think you love me too. And I get why that terrifies you."

"It doesn't terrify me."

"Bullshit." He fired that out like a bullet. Relentless, his aim true. "It scares you so badly you'd do anything to run away from it. And I sympathize, I do. The last time you fell in love it ended badly and this time you sure weren't looking for anything. But the thing is, darlin', you don't get to choose."

She felt as if her skin was too small, stretched across her bones until she was practically see-through. She felt vulnerable. Exposed.

It should have been unbearable.

She waited for the shame to kick in, but it didn't. She

waited for the grief to come claim her, but there was nothing there. Just that same old sadness, more sweet than bitter these days, she imagined she would always carry with her. Somewhere deep inside.

"I think you're wrong," she said, almost solemnly. "I think you do get to choose."

Something ignited inside of him then. She saw it. She felt it. His eyes kindled with a bright flame and his hard mouth went tight.

"You were right about me," he told her, fiercely. "I'm a martyr and I'm a dick. And I've been proud of both for so long that I don't know any different. Until you. Don't you understand? I didn't see you coming either."

She whispered his name, but he ignored it, moving in even closer until he took over the whole saloon. Or maybe the world.

"You make me wish I was a better man," Cody told her, as if he was making vows. "You make me think I could be, if I wanted. If I tried. And Skylar, you must know you're the only thing on this earth that could ever make me want to try."

"Cody," she tried again.

"And I know you left me because you think you're still in pieces." He reached out and slid his hand over her jaw, curling his fingers around the base of her skull and pulling her face to his. "But you are not broken."

She might not have been broken, but she couldn't seem

to stop the tears that welled up and started down her cheeks at that. Not because she was sad. It was a different emotion entirely. Complex. Layered.

And it had everything to do with the hard man in front of her.

"Everybody's scarred, darlin'," he told her, his voice almost hoarse, as if the things he was saying were as difficult for him as they were for her. Difficult and good, she thought. Difficult and necessary. "It's what makes you strong. It's nothing to be ashamed of. The fact that you can get up again and move on? That's what makes you beautiful, Skylar. It's what makes you *you*."

"You need to stop talking," she told him then. She wiped at her cheeks and saw something bleak move over his face, like a cold shadow. And she smiled at him then, no matter if her cheeks were damp. "I was just standing here thinking about how easy it was going to be to stalk you, after this weekend. And figuring exactly how I was going to do it. Sacramento, San Diego, Tucson. So many options to hunt you down on tour."

He blinked. For a moment his dark green eyes looked blank. Then slowly, very slowly, the corner of his mouth kicked up.

And all those knotted things inside of Skylar seemed to run smooth.

"I'm glad to hear that," he said slowly, as if he was picturing all the things he could do with her in all those places.

His hand tightened just a little bit on her neck. "And it's okay if you don't know how you feel, baby. I'm a bull rider. I like a challenge. Give me enough time, and I promise, I'll make you love me. I'll make you forget."

There was a time she might have heard that as a threat. Found it offensive, even. But tonight, she reached over and put her hands on him, reveling in the flat planes of his sculpted chest.

Letting the heat of him remind her that she hadn't been anything like frozen in some time.

"I'm never going to forget him," she said, soft and sure. And she held Cody's gaze because she wanted to make certain he understood. "Because remembering Thayer reminds me of the girl who fell in love with him. I'm always going to think about her, and wonder who she would have been if he'd lived." When he started to say something, she let her fingers curl into fists, and gripped him a little harder. "But she's not me, Cody. She died when he did and I'm not the same person as I was then. I can never be that person again."

She took a deep breath, held on to him, and kept going.

"This is who I am." She tipped her head back and smiled at him, damp cheeks and all. "I'm the girl who fell in love the minute I opened my father's door and let you in. I'm the girl who slept with a stranger on a picnic table and somehow never felt cheap. You've seen me messy, real, and a little bit crazy. You've seen me lie and you've seen me run and you didn't let me hide. You drove all the way here because I somehow 'forgot' to give you my number."

"I love you," he said again, as if it was a challenge. One he intended to win.

"It's not that you know me in ways he never did, you know a different person. He was the right man for someone who doesn't exist anymore. You're the right man for me." She laughed a little bit at that. Because this should feel crazy. This should feel like silly, giddy madness that might disappear at any moment. And yet, somehow, it didn't. It felt as solid as the wall behind her that had stood there since the 1880s. It felt as real as Marietta. "Although it's only been three weeks. I guess that could change."

"Strap in, darlin'," Cody said in his low, determined way that made her heart flip over in her chest. "Because it's not going to change. I'm pretty sure this is it."

"I love how your version of romance is always a threat," Skylar said, then she let out a little squeal, because he was moving again.

He pulled her into his arms, and then he dipped her low. As if they were in a very old movie. The kind of movie that would be filmed in black-and-white and take place in a saloon just like this one. He dipped her down, over his arm, like some kind of ballroom dance. He dipped her down until she thought her head might hit the floor behind her, or would have, if she didn't trust him to hold her up. He dipped her until she felt as if she must have been wearing some kind of ball gown, when she knew better. When she knew that she was wearing a cute little sundress and matching sweater, like the conservative and sweet thing she didn't think she was anymore.

Or wasn't around him, anyway.

Cody dipped her until she was certain every single eye in the room was on them, if they hadn't been already.

"Say it," he ordered her, that glittering thing in his dark green eyes that made her tremble. Everywhere. "Or I swear I'll drop you on the floor."

"I love you," she told him, unable to contain her smile. "And you're not going to drop me. Just think how that would play on social media. Can't ride a bull, can't dip a girl—"

"It's that mouth," he said then, as if in some kind of wonder. "That crooked smile. And someday, Skylar, the only ghost you'll have in your eyes will be me."

And when he kissed her, she saw fireworks all over again, though this time she knew that they were inside. And it wasn't the Fourth of July.

It was just him.

And it took her longer than it should have to understand that it was her family, cheering them on, as if the famous Grey Curse was shattering all around them.

But none of that mattered. Because all she felt, all she wanted, was Cody.

For as long as she could have him.

Chapter Fourteen

CODY SPENT THE remainder of his last American Extreme Bull Riders Tour with his very own buckle bunny, who theatrically programmed her number into his phone that very same night in Marietta. Skylar slept in his trailer and she cheered for him in the stands, and when he officially retired at the championship show in Fort Worth that October, hers was the only voice he could hear in all that cheering.

Hers was the only voice he wanted to hear.

And then he was done with bulls and all his endless injuries and ready for the ride of his life.

He started with a wedding, marrying Skylar in Montana with her family all around and his in awe, where it had all began.

"I love you," he told her that night, when she was finally his wife, out beneath the stars.

"I know," she replied, and then laughed when he nipped her chin. "I love you too, Cody. So much it hurts."

It was the only way he ever wanted to hurt her.

They built a house that sprawled there on that California

bluff where they'd sat in camp chairs in front of his Airstream, with a wide porch that they could sit on when the weather was right. They watched hundreds of sunsets right there, huddled together in the same chair, the way they had back then. They built a little ranch that turned into something bigger on some of that land, raising cattle and sheep and breeding a few prize bulls with that American Extreme star quality written all over them. Cody didn't miss riding—he liked walking without pain too much and life without concussions—but he sure liked imagining Galen bulls tossing new bull riders straight off into the dirt.

He liked that a lot.

He put his sisters through college and let them come and live in the ranch's guesthouse when they needed it, because being around all those Greys over the years made him rethink his definition of family and closeness and what that meant to everybody involved. So much so that when his mother finally left Todd, a few years after Kathleen graduated from Vanderbilt, he gave her his old Airstream and let her live in it on his property. In a private little grove near the sea, to let the Pacific help her heal.

In time Skylar gave him a son, a squalling little alien creature they both loved so much it should have terrified him. Sometimes Cody thought it did. And they named him after the men they'd lost, Charlie Galen and Thayer Sexton, because neither one of them believed in walking shrines, but their whole, sweet life was about second chances.

And little Charlie Thayer Galen was hope made real, and a yeller.

But he was as stubborn as his mama and as determined as his father, so Cody wasn't entirely surprised when little Charlie, at all of six years old, demanded that he get to ride bulls like his daddy.

"Tell me this is a phase," Skylar murmured as Charlie demonstrated what he'd learned from watching videos of Cody.

All over the living room furniture. Making his three-year-old brother Grey shriek with delight and chase around after him.

But Cody saw the jut of his son's chin. And that faraway look in his green eyes. He recognized it, even in a six-year-old.

He grinned at his wife. Not exactly sheepishly, because he wasn't the one who'd showed the kids his videos.

And Skylar shook her head, sitting there like she wasn't his whole world, with their five-month-old daughter Cady snug in her arms and all that love all over her face.

That tried and tested love, as sweet as the day she'd swung open the door to her father's house in Billings and changed them both forever. The kind of love that redeemed a dick like Cody and saved them both from their darker impulses of whiskey and grief and loneliness. Three kids and still so much laughter—that kind of love. The things she whispered to him in the dark when she moved over him in their bedroom with its sturdy lock on the door. The things he promised her when she was clenched tight around him, still calling him *oh God.*

All this love that was theirs, miraculous and impossible, hard and soft, as loud as it was quiet and spun out over all these years. The fights that ended in wild make-up sex and the other ones that ended with both of them feeling so fragile, only resolve and forgiveness and a little bit of bull-headedness got them through.

The roar of it. The endless dance, jolts and bumps and a header into the dirt, only to climb back up to their feet to do it all over again.

And again and again and again.

Cody looked at her beautiful face, more beautiful now that he knew her better than he knew himself sometimes and no more ghosts between them, and he wouldn't change a thing.

"I guess I brought this on myself," Skylar said, as if she knew what he was thinking, out here on their bluff so many miles away from everything, with only the sea and the stars she loved as witness. "I knew who I married."

Cody caught each of his sons in one arm, lifting them off the floor to make them howl with glee, and he looked at his women. The wife he loved more than any other person alive, and the little girl he was already certain he'd happily kill for, if necessary.

This longest, best ride. His life.

"It will be fine, darlin'," he promised her. And then he smiled, because he knew he'd make sure that it was, or die trying. "Trust me."

The End

The American Extreme Bull Riders Tour

If you enjoyed *Cody*, you'll love the rest of the American Extreme Bull Riders Tour!

Book 1: *Tanner* by Sarah Mayberry

Book 2: *Chase* by Barbara Dunlop

Book 3: *Casey* by Kelly Hunter

Book 4: *Cody* by Megan Crane

Book 5: *Troy* by Amy Andrews

Book 6: *Kane* by Sinclair Jayne

Book 7: *Austin* by Jeannie Watt

Book 8: *Gage* by Katherine Garbera

Available now at your favorite online retailer!

Want to know more about The Greys?

The Greys of Montana

Christina Grey's story

Book 1: *Come Home for Christmas, Cowboy*

Jesse Grey's story

Book 2: *In Bed with the Bachelor*

Scottie Grey's story

Book 3: *Project Virgin*

Available now at your favorite online retailer!

About the Author

USA Today bestselling, RITA-nominated, and critically-acclaimed author **Megan Crane** has written more than fifty books since her debut in 2004. She has been published by a variety of publishers, including each of New York's Big Five. She's won fans with her women's fiction, chick lit, and work-for-hire young adult novels as well as with the Harlequin Presents she writes as **Caitlin Crews**. These days her focus is on contemporary romance from small town to international glamor, cowboys to bikers, and beyond. She sometimes teaches creative writing classes both online at media-bistro.com and at UCLA Extension's prestigious Writers' Program, where she finally utilizes the MA and PhD in English Literature she received from the University of York in York, England. She currently lives in the Pacific Northwest with a husband who draws comics and animation storyboards and their menagerie of ridiculous animals.

Thank you for reading

Cody

If you enjoyed this book, you can find more from all our great authors at TulePublishing.com, or from your favorite online retailer.

Made in the USA
San Bernardino, CA
06 May 2019